Rules For Dating

Harriet Evans is the author of seven previous novels: *Going Home, A Hopeless Romantic, The Love of Her Life, I Remember You, Love Always, Happily Ever After* and *Not Without You.* She lives in London with her family.

Also by Harriet Evans

Going Home
A Hopeless Romantic
The Love of Her Life
I Remember You
Love Always
Happily Ever After
Not Without You

Rules For Dating a Romantic Hero

Harriet Evans

HARPER

Harper
An imprint of HarperCollins*Publishers*
77–85 Fulham Palace Road,
Hammersmith, London W6 8JB

www.harpercollins.co.uk

First published in Great Britain by
HarperCollins*Publishers* 2014

A catalogue record for this book is
available from the British Library

ISBN: 978-0-00-754536-0

Typeset in ITC Stone Serif by Palimpsest Book Production Ltd,
Falkirk, Stirlingshire

MIX
Paper from
responsible sources
FSC® C007454

FSC™ is a non-profit international organisation established to promote
the responsible management of the world's forests. Products carrying the
FSC label are independently certified to assure consumers that they come
from forests that are managed to meet the social, economic and
ecological needs of present and future generations,
and other controlled sources.

Find out more about HarperCollins and the environment at
www.harpercollins.co.uk/green

'In the company of an unmarried couple it is impolite to ask when they will be announcing their engagement.'

Ronald Twistleton-Smythe's Guide to Modern Manners, 1926

From the *Daily News*, Friday 6 July 2012:

Good news for everyone who misses their weekly fix of *Downton Abbey*: the real-life version is about to get interesting. Those in the Norfolk area on Saturday lunchtime should hurry along to Chartley Hall, one of England's greatest stately homes. It is the family seat of dashing, brooding Dominic, Marquis of Ranelagh (regularly voted the UK's most eligible bachelor). The house is without a mistress, but, my sources say, not for long. The Marquis, also known as Nick, has been dating 'ordinary' girl Laura Foster, whom he met when she visited the house with her parents four years ago. Theirs has been a stormy relationship, to say the least, with Laura furious at the lack of wedding bells. But I hear things could be about to change. The Marquis has funded Laura's very own pet project, a children's bookshop in the village. It opens this weekend with speeches and a hog roast and, we presume, a rare sighting of the elusive couple. Will Laura get the one thing she's been wishing for . . . a ring?

Rule One:

Shoot anyone who compares you to Kate Middleton

Sometimes, Laura found her situation funny. Most of the time it was wonderful, if pretty weird. But sometimes there were moments when she'd have to bite the inside of her mouth to stop herself from laughing. She'd close her eyes and wish her flatmate Paddy could see her judge the Cutest Pug Competition. Or her best friend Jo could watch her come down the stairs of Chartley in a long ballgown, curtseying to a Very Important Royal Person.

After the moment was over she'd allow herself a small grin, nothing more in case anyone was watching. Because she was the only one who seemed to think it was completely bloody crackers that she, Laura Foster, was living this life. She had literally nothing to her name (unless you counted her 'Friend to Animals' Brownie badge and her First Prize for

Best Doodle at St Mark's Primary School, 1989).

There was only one reason for it, too, and that was Nick. She had realised a while ago that being with Nick meant she had to give up a lot, but it was always going to be worth it.

She'd said this to Jo once, sitting outside the pub, glugging white wine spritzers. Jo had swallowed an ice cube and nearly choked to death.

'Give up a lot?' she'd said after a few minutes, once the colour in her face had returned to (nearly) normal. 'That's blimmin' rich! Quite literally! Get over it, Laura, what are you on about?'

Laura had swirled her glass around so the ice clanked loudly, like chains. 'It sounds stupid, forget it. But there is stuff you give up,' she said. 'It's hard to explain.'

'What exactly? Spending your own money? Living in a hovel? You are funny, Laura. If I were you I'd give up living with Paddy and doing your job in a heartbeat.' Jo was down to earth. 'God, I'd give up being married to Chris and having Iris if it meant shacking up with Nick in his house. Most people would. You're Kate Bloody Middleton!'

Then Jo leaned forward, breathing wine

fumes into Laura's face. 'Don't go around complaining. It makes you sound like one of the ugly sisters out of *Cinderella*. I mean, 'cos of the complaining, not 'cos you're ugly.'

Laura had laughed and said, 'Of course. You're right, I should shut up.' And she didn't talk to Jo about it again.

After all, these little things that worried her more and more lately – they were just in her head, weren't they? Why couldn't she just forget about the annoying stuff and enjoy the rest of it? Pretend her life was as perfect as everyone assumed it was? Like Mum and Dad's neighbours, whom she'd bump into on the high street back home. Or her work mates who thought the whole thing was hilarious – 'Where's Laura? Entertaining the King of Denmark this weekend?' Or her old friends who'd started off thinking it was mad and now thought it was great. And it was, wasn't it? Why on earth wouldn't it be?

But Nick and Laura's relationship wasn't great. She didn't know why, she just knew things weren't right. And they hadn't been for a while, really, not since . . . well, it was hard to say when. She thought that maybe he was still angry with her for what she'd done. Or that she regretted coming back to him. On the surface, everything continued as normal. She could forget about it most of the time, pretend it was all in her head.

Perhaps it all really started the day of the grand opening of the bookshop.

Rule Two:

Real-life romantic heroes come with real-life families. And families are like neighbours – you're stuck with them. Make the best of it.

'Laura, dear. You look lovely. I'm sorry to disturb . . .' Lady Rose Balmore, Nick's elder sister, came into the bedroom (without knocking – she never knocked). She gave Laura a brief smile as she bustled past her and flung open one of the small cupboards in the eaves of the roof.

'I am sure there's a pair of candlesticks in here that would be perfect in the Green Chamber. We put them away when all the work was done, and Tony's convinced they belong downstairs again. You don't mind me looking, do you?'

Laura paused in the act of picking paint out

of her hair. She'd been up 'til 2 a.m. the previous night at the bookshop. 'Go ahead,' she said, even though Rose was already rifling through the cupboard. 'Be my guest.'

Downstairs a loud bell sounded and Rose stood up. 'Aha! Opening time.' She cocked her head. 'My favourite moment of the day.'

Every morning, come rain or shine, every day of the year (except Christmas and New Year's Day) a bell would ring at 10 a.m. to declare Chartley Hall open for business. From Nick's small, sunny bedroom, right at the top of the vast building, Laura could look out and see the visitors arriving. Cars crawling up the long avenue of oaks, cameras and phones snapping away. Men, women and children in their hundreds swarming across the terrace, up the great front stairs, marching out across the vast back lawn where teas were served.

Sometimes Laura would emerge from Nick's private quarters onto the main corridor of the house and people would stare at her in surprise. Who was this person, coming out of a secret doorway? Was it a . . . a real-life *aristocrat*? Then they'd examine her more closely, and either look away or move on. Oh no, she's one of us. Doesn't belong here. Lost her way probably. It made her smile that it was so obvious to them.

Of course, if she happened to be walking through the house with Nick, it was a different story. People stopped and stared and giggled, as if David Beckham, Colin Firth and Prince William all rolled into one had suddenly appeared in front of them. Rose, Nick's other sister Lavinia, or their still-glamorous mother Vivienne all got the same reaction. The Needhams were a good-looking bunch, even if, like Nick, they either didn't know or didn't care.

There was just *something* about them. Their mother had been a film star and their father came from a family as old as the Wars of the Roses. Though Laura thought that was all rubbish – didn't everyone come from someone who was alive several hundred years ago? And it was hardly like they were perfect, either.

Rose had – though to mention it was to bring on a stare so cold it could freeze Hell – an early marriage to a rock star and a stretch in rehab for heroin addiction under her belt. These never seemed to come up when she was making speeches to the Women's Institute on Living in the World's Most Beautiful House. No, it was very much part of the past, and not to be discussed.

Laura sometimes like to remind herself of

it, though, when Rose said something particularly *Daily Mail*-ish. Nick's family had a happy knack for rewriting history, which was good, because they'd been around so long Laura supposed you couldn't always be raking up old mistakes.

Recently, now that both of Rose's children were away at boarding school and her husband Sir Malcolm was often abroad on business trips, she'd been spending more than half her time at Chartley Hall.

'Good morning!' she'd say, sweeping past a gaggle of bug-eyed pensioners kitted out in all-weather mackintoshes. 'Have a wonderful day! I see you have a guide to the gardens. May I recommend the pergola? It's so pleasant this time of year.'

If the world was fairer, or if they were all living in Sweden, Rose would have inherited the house, and maybe she'd have been the best person for the job. She did really love it. Maybe too much. Laura watched her now as she gazed out of the window, fingers drumming on the wide ledge, absorbed by the view of the park, the curve of the East Wing of the house, then tore herself away, turning back towards Laura.

'Are we all ready?' Rose gave her a bright

smile. 'Is it . . . ah. Are you wearing that for the opening?'

Laura looked down at her khaki silk Topshop button-down shirtdress. 'Yes. Er, I bought it specially.'

'Right. Right, wonderful!'

'Rose,' Laura said. 'What does that mean?'

'I only thought you might want to wear something more traditional.' Rose cleared her throat delicately. 'This is your big day. Of sorts.'

'What's the traditional dress for opening a children's bookshop?' Laura said, trying to sound jokey. 'Harry Potter scar'n'specs? Mog? Meg?' She knew she was rambling, she always did when she was nervous. 'The other Mog, I always think it's weird that there are two different cats called—'

'Yes, yes,' Rose said sharply. She moved towards Laura, smoothing her pale pink Chanel suit over her hips with brisk efficiency. 'You know, dear, you have to stop going off the point. Nick's spent a lot setting you up in this business. People are going to be watching you today.' One neat finger flicked a brave lock of bobbed hair out of her face. 'Please don't let him down.'

'He didn't set me up, I applied for the grant and the Foundation gave it to me . . .' Laura began, then stopped.

'Nearly all the funding – you still have to get the final piece,' said Rose briskly. 'And, of course, I'm *sure* you will.'

Laura shrugged and smiled, determined on this, of all days, not to let Rose wind her up. 'Come now. Less Lady Thatcher, eh? Today's a celebration.'

Rose closed her eyes, just briefly, and smiled. 'Of course. Perhaps I shouldn't have said it. We're all so proud of you. This bookshop's a wonderful thing for the village. For the whole estate. I should leave you to do your make-up.'

She patted her on the arm graciously and left Laura, who had just spent ten minutes doing her make-up, staring at herself in the mirror.

Breathe deeply. It's going to be great. Had the carpet fitter fixed the metal trim that Casey had tripped over only yesterday? Had the wholesaler delivered the last of the Peppa Pig books? Would the paint be dry? If the paint wasn't dry and people started sitting down on windowsills it would be a disaster, a huge, mega, painted-bottoms disaster. *Breathe . . .*

The door opened again and she whirled round, hoping it would be him.

'Can I borrow Ma's necklace, Laura?' Lavinia, Nick's younger sister, wafted in on a cloud of heavy perfume, her long boho skirt swishing, her anklet bracelets jangling lightly. On her hip was a small, grubby child, Egg. 'Oh and Nick said it'd be OK if I took that quilt? It'd look great in the cottage. Plus it's so cold in there, you know? No big deal, but it really is cold in there.'

Laura said, 'Hi, Egg. Hi, Lavinia. The necklace is in the safe. You'll have to ask Nick.'

'But you wore it last week, haven't you still got it?'

Breathe. 'No. It's a diamond necklace, Lav. I've only ever worn it that once. He doesn't let me keep it on the chest of drawers in the saucer with my Accessorize plastic diamond earrings, you know.'

Lavinia put her head on one side and stared at Laura, her pale blue eyes drifting over Laura's dress. 'He lets you wear it, though. It's not fair, I mean, that was Mum's necklace.'

It wasn't your mother's, Laura thought. It's the estate's. I'm not trying to steal it. It was really heavy and the clasp gave me a blister and besides, it's not actually that relaxing wearing thousands of pounds round your neck like some show pony. Not for the first time, Laura wished Nick was here. No one ever seemed to try it on when he was around.

'Sorry. Look, Lav, I have to go and make sure everything's OK before the opening, so . . .'

'That's a great dress, is it Marc Jacobs?'

'It's from Topshop,' Laura said. 'The only thing I can afford from Marc Jacobs is a plastic bag.'

'Right. He doesn't actually do plastic bags. OK. Well . . .' Her eyes strayed round the room, like a lazy magpie.

'Have you seen Nick?', Laura said hurriedly. 'He was up so early this morning I missed him.'

Lavinia shook her head. 'No. But Charles said they had some project. They've been in his study for hours. He's exhausted. There's so much going on at the moment, isn't there?'

'Er . . . yes,' Laura said vaguely. The truth was Nick had been so wrapped up in the house lately, closeted away with Charles, full of plans, and she wasn't part of them. The finances of Chartley, not great since his money-wasting father's death, were more worrying than ever thanks to mortgages, insurance premiums and the modernising of the estate. 'I don't really know what's up.' She felt that she could at least talk to Lavinia about things. 'I feel bad. I've been so busy with the shop that I haven't really asked him about it.'

'Right. Egg, don't bite Mummy, OK? You look great, Laura. Oh, I meant to ask? What's the free book situation, by the way? Just let me know when you know.' Lavinia bent forward and suddenly kissed Laura, 'Well done. You're such a clever girl, I honestly don't know how you do it. See you later.'

Laura was left facing the door.

She turned back, looking herself over one more time with a sigh. Why did her dresses always crumple the moment she put them on? Why was her hair already greasy? Then she took another deep breath. You're a real person. You've got a proper job working four days a week for the council, for God's sake. This book-shop is another job. So that makes two more jobs than Lavinia or Rose have, unless you count butting in as a job, in which case, yes, they have full-time jobs—

The door swung open again. 'Yes?' she almost snarled.

'Hello, Laura.' Nick stood in the doorway and her heart jumped at the sight of him. He paused at the door, looking at her, then shut it quietly. She thought with a pang how tired he looked.

He was always tired these days. 'I'm sorry I missed you this morning.' He came towards her and took her in his arms. 'You look gorgeous.'

'I'm glad you're here.' She inhaled the smell of him – sweet, hay-like sweat, something spicy. 'Everything all right?'

'Sure.' He nodded. 'All set for today?'

'Oh yes. Your sisters are both on excellent form, by the way.'

Nick kissed her. 'Forget about them.' He stroked her cheek. She loved the feeling of his body against hers, his comforting, muscular solidity.

'It's jolly hard to when they stroll in while you're getting dressed. Can't we get a lock for the door?'

'Rose only wanted the candlesticks,' he said into her hair.

Laura stepped back. 'Aha, she didn't actually. She came in to check on me. Make sure I wasn't wearing something stupid.'

Nick sighed. 'She means well.'

'No she doesn't!'

He laughed. 'You're right. She means unwell. Never mind. I love you.'

'I love you, too.' She kissed him, his jaw, his nose, his lips.

'Can we start season three of *The Sopranos* tonight?'

'You bet.' She gripped his shoulders. 'Nick, thank you for today. For everything.'

He looked at her, almost amazed. 'Why? It was your idea. You got the funding, you found the place. You've done everything while still doing that other job back in London. You're incredible.'

'I'm not. And we don't know if it's going to work.'

'It will work. That's what I've been talking to Charles about. The estate's changing. We need to plan for the future. Find other reasons for people to come here, and you're a main part of that.'

For some silly reason, Laura could feel her heart thumping in her chest. 'Me?'

'I mean the shop. Not you. I know you hate all that stuff.' He sounded so businesslike. She was oddly shy then, and glad when he pulled her towards him again, and kissed her gently. 'You can do anything, Laura. And this is your thing.'

They stepped apart, still smiling stupidly at each other. She grabbed her shoes and bag and the two of them walked out together, down the winding old staircase and out onto the corridor, hung with portraits of Nick's ancestors. Laura gazed up at a Van Dyck portrait of

17

Lady Sybil Needham. She'd taken over the running of the estate and then moved to Paris in her old age, marrying a man thirty years her junior. Hello old girl, she thought, staring at the poised figure with the serious eyes and clever face. I've always rather liked the look of you.

The first group of tourists stopped and stared.

'Oh my God, it's you,' a woman in her fifties carrying a camera and a guide book, said. 'Gosh. I'm sorry!' She laughed, near-hysterical. 'So good to see you!'

'Hello,' said Nick. 'Er, you too!' He shoved his hands in his pockets. 'Everything OK? I hope you're enjoying yourselves.'

'We're having a wonderful time,' said her friend, who had severely bobbed grey hair. 'Absolutely marvellous. Everyone says it, but you don't believe it 'til you're here. This really is the most beautiful house we have, isn't it?'

'Well,' Nick said, putting his hand on the small of Laura's back, 'I think so.'

The two of them glanced in surprise at Laura by his side. 'Well, lovely,' said the first, uncertainly.

'My girlfriend's opening a children's book-shop in the village this afternoon,' Nick said.

18

'We're on our way there now. You should drop by, it's wonderful. Excuse me.'

They smiled, but their expression was curious. 'Right. Thank you,' the first one said. She looked Laura over, rather disappointed. 'How nice for you, dear,' she said vaguely. 'Marjorie, let's be moving on.'

'I think she was hoping for a character from *Downton Abbey* instead of me,' said Laura as she and Nick emerged into the Great Hall and walked across the black and white marble flooring, taken from a Roman palace.

'You're exaggerating,' Nick said. 'She just wished you weren't there. Or dead.' He held the door open and she passed through, down the golden stone steps, and the visitors who were just arriving stopped and stared.

'Welcome to Chartley Hall,' Nick said, holding the door open for them and smiling in a friendly way. 'Thanks so much for coming to our home. Have a fantastic time.'

'That lady he's with, she's the girlfriend from nowhere,' she heard one of them say as they walked away. 'I read about her in the paper last week.'

'She's from Middlesex or something isn't she?' another one put in. She could feel their eyes on her back. 'Her dad's a handyman or

19

something. Do you know they couldn't even afford to go abroad when she was a kid? They had a caravan. I read that somewhere.'

'Well, she's got her claws into this one, hasn't she? Good for her.'

Rule Three:

Get a good answer ready for those questions about wedding bells.

'It's not easy, being the girlfriend of the most eligible bachelor in the whole country. After Prince William, that is, and he's out of the running now!' The crowd gave an excited laugh. You could sense them thinking: At last. Someone's mentioned it! Rose, in her absolute element at the microphone, gave a wicked chuckle. 'They're pretending not to hear me. Well, big sisters are supposed to embarrass their little brothers, aren't they?'

Laura shot a glance at Nick out of the corner of her eye, but his gaze was fixed firmly to the floor. In front of them was the shop, its new sign bold green and white:

Laura's Place
A bookshop for children and their grown-ups

Once again, Laura wished her parents were here. But she'd been too – shy? Worried? – to invite them, and they'd come down the previous weekend instead to see the shop. It was stupid, because they'd have loved it. They were so proud of her, getting this whole thing off the ground. If the rest of her life baffled them, this, at least, was something they could entirely get their heads round and tell their neighbours about.

'It's hard, dear, knowing what to say to people. I don't like to brag about it. After all,' her mother had said, without meaning to sound unkind. 'What is there to brag about? You're not married to him. He just happens to be . . .' And she'd trailed off.

He just happened to be Dominic Edward Danvers Needham, twelfth Marquis of Ranelagh, Earl of Albany Cross, Lord of the Handfast, owner of Chartley Hall and 10,000 acres of land. Title created over 600 years ago after the Wars of the Roses. House designed by Inigo Jones. The finest collection of Renaissance drawings in the country. A muster of peacocks (yes, after three years, she knew what the name

22

for a group of peacocks was). And a diamond tiara worn by Queen Victoria during her first tour of India. To say nothing of the castle in Scotland, the properties in London, the diamonds and other jewels residing in the vault, the foundation that gave away millions of pounds in grants every year.

And she just happened to be a normal girl – nothing more, nothing less – from a London suburb, a house with a rusty climbing frame in the garden, a caravan, enough money for new shoes, but not enough money for holidays abroad. A safe life, a boring life, a happy life.

When she'd told her parents what she was planning, her mother had clapped her hands together. 'Well, Laura, that's great! Good for you. We were worried . . .' She'd glanced at her husband, who'd stared into his newspaper as though it held the secret to the location of the lost city of Atlantis. 'We were worried you might not have anything up there that's your own.'

'Oh,' Laura had said, a little puzzled.

Then Angela Foster had said, 'It's such a big place. And to me you still seem . . . so small.' She had laughed, tears in her eyes, and Laura had suddenly found herself struggling not to cry as well. 'I just . . . well, I'm very glad you're doing that. We're very proud of you.'

Laura had spent nearly ten years working on volunteer reading programmes for a local London council, and Laura's Place was her long-term dream come true. A place for children to flick through all the books they wanted. A playground, with cabins at the back of the garden. There was room to sleep up to twenty children at a time. Eventually the old school house, which had been turned into a shop, would also become a centre where kids from all over the country, especially deprived areas or families where English wasn't their first language, could come for a weekend. To learn about the joy of books, camping, bonfires and games on the estate. Each child would be given a bag of books and a mentor to stay in touch with afterwards.

She hoped to replicate Laura's Place elsewhere in a couple of years, but that was the next stage. She was waiting for the final funding to come through from a few sources, including the Needham Trust, the charitable foundation run by Nick's family which, like many charities, could only give away so much each year.

The following weekend, she and Nick had agreed to an interview with Laura's greatest enemy, the *Daily News*, who were obsessed with her and her relationship with Nick. One of the advisors who'd helped set up the shop had arranged it. 'You have to do it. It's a talking point, to promote the shop and secure that last piece of funding. You have to sound credible. Happy. Together. Committed.'

She loved that. *Committed!*

The old red brick gleamed, the green front door and white windows sparkled with fresh (dry) paint. Inside the shop was stacked with shelves and brightly coloured furniture, bean bags, cushions and mats, so anyone could sit on the floor and read.

Casey, the manager, was a local single mother of two. Brian, the vicar's husband who was an ex-teacher, was now part-time bookshop assistant. Both stood proudly beside Laura. They were all exhausted. Nick took the microphone from his sister Rose.

'Thank you, Rose. I won't keep you, ladies, gentlemen and children.' He grinned. 'This is a wonderful day for Chartley. For us, and for a generation of children who are going to enjoy this shop. It's all because of Laura, and I want to raise a glass to her and tell her . . .'

She lifted her eyes to his, but her smile froze when she saw his expression. She followed his gaze as a slim blonde girl in a white kaftan, jeans and thong sandals, standing slightly apart from the group, waved shyly at him and let her hand slide quickly back to her side.

Laura recognised her but couldn't place her. Nick looked ruffled, dumbstruck, even. Whoever she was, he didn't want her here, that was for sure.

Laura nudged him, and he shook his head and continued.

'I . . . I've forgotten what I was going to say. To Laura's Place! Oh! Hog roast starting in a few minutes, and please go into the shop and have a look round, buy something, enjoy yourselves. Thank you.'

The local and national journalists in the front row shuffled in annoyance. 'Nick, smile for the camera please,' said the largest one, a beefy, red-faced guy. 'Laura, get close to him, please.'

'Me, too?' said Rose, edging towards them.

'No thanks. Just one of the happy couple. You know what I mean,' said the photographer as a couple of people sniggered. Laura and Nick stood still, like waxworks in a museum, and when she glanced up again, the girl in white had disappeared. It was then that Laura remembered who she was. Nick's ex-girlfriend, Lara Montagu.

They'd never really discussed Lara. It was in the past, but it was also too recent. It was one of the things she and Nick didn't talk about.

Rule Four:

Don't Google yourself, and don't read newspapers.

She struggled sometimes to remember what the old Laura had been like. The one who'd met Nick nearly four years ago, in a field behind the woods at the back of Chartley Hall. She had reasonably assumed that this tall, muscular man driving a mower was someone who worked on the estate. That girl had probably been pretty normal, Laura thought now, but back then her life seemed to be a total mess. At twenty-six, she fell in love all the time, and she could never seem to see the flaws everyone else did. The guys were gay, they were crazy, they were engaged, or they kept promising to leave their girlfriend, who then turned out to be pregnant.

It was after this, her most recent (and most catastrophic) romantic disaster, that Laura had found herself up in Norfolk staying with her parents at her grandmother's house by the sea. It was almost a working holiday. Time for her to work out what she was doing wrong, that is: why she kept looking for romantic heroes and ending up with losers. Years of Jane Austen TV dramas and slushy novels about tall, dark, handsome men with curt manners and amazing kissing techniques had twisted her perspective. She'd decided she had to reject everything to do with romance.

Then she met Nick. Who, it turned out later, wasn't a farmhand, but one of those bloody romantic heroes, a character from a novel come to life.

But the thing was, it was wonderful – all the time, either when they were alone in her crummy flat or hanging out in London with her friends. She was completely, totally happy when she was with Nick, and he was with her. So many men before had wanted only the best bits of her, or to change her. Nick wanted her to be as much like herself as possible.

He wanted to watch TV with her and join in hilariously with her attempts to bake (everyone was baking, so Laura thought she ought to try it). He wanted to sit up with Paddy, Laura's hapless flatmate, listening to the traumatic stories of his relationship breakdown. He wanted to lie in bed with her, tracing the edge of her hand with his finger, or read her stories from the papers on Saturday mornings or sing her Johnny Cash songs in his special growly voice.

But that was in London. Up at Chartley Hall things weren't the same, and that's when it started to go wrong.

Eighteen months into their relationship, Laura was offered the job of a lifetime, working in San Francisco for a tech company developing children's reading programmes. At first she'd told them she wasn't interested. But the more she protested that she didn't want to leave, the more she realised she had to. She had to give Nick a fresh start, a chance to meet someone new who'd be exactly what he needed. Not the person she'd become when she was at Chartley: stilted, nervous, not herself.

She still remembered Nick's face when she'd told him she was leaving.

'You know this place, it isn't me, Laura,' he'd said, his dark eyes liquid, his jaw set. 'None of this matters. We matter. You and me. You can't go.'

'You said that before,' she'd replied, holding his hand – his dear, sweet, warm hand that was strong and gentle – and her heart felt as though it would actually break, it hurt so much. 'You said that when we got together, and it wasn't true. It *does* matter.'

'You're wrong. What can I do to change your mind?'

But Laura couldn't say, Give up Chartley Hall, let's live somewhere else. Tell your sister Rose to leave me alone. It was her own fault she couldn't make this work, her fault she constantly forgot the names of important people, or broke plates, or opened the door the wrong way on Tony the butler, giving him a black eye, or annoyed the staff by going down to the kitchen and making a cup of tea at night. It was her fault she still didn't understand the strange rules and traditions.

Laura had really snapped the week before at the county show and told the reporter from the *Norfolk Gazette* that of course she was a feminist and didn't understand why, if they were going to pass a law so that eldest daughters could become queen, they couldn't do the same for peers of the realm. Laura thought this was a perfectly normal thing to think: after all, wasn't it 2010?

But the headline in the newspaper (next to 'Lowestoft: 200 Tonnes of Horse Manure Catches Alight') was 'Lord's New Ladyfriend:

Man-hating Revolutionary?' Which, as Nick pointed out, was a bit of a contradiction: how could you be a Lord's ladyfriend and a man-hater at the same time?

Rose also made it quite clear that Laura didn't cut the mustard. Rose was there on the terrible night that Laura dropped the Wedgwood plate worth thousands of pounds. As Laura stood in the ballroom in despair, while Tony donned gloves and swept the pieces carefully up into a special polystyrene box ready to be mended, she actually said, 'Laura, dear, where you come from it's normal to pick up objects and touch them. Here, we don't do that. Please be more careful with my family's things in future.'

My family's things.

There would be dinners with other posh people, and Laura would sit and watch, not knowing what to say, while girls like Lara Montagu, one of Nick's oldest childhood friends, with her perfect white teeth, thick blonde hair, clear skin and total, one hundred per cent confidence would laugh and joke with each other. Lara even had a degree in Marketing and Estate Management; she might as well have had 'Ideal Wife' stamped on her forehead.

And Laura would think, You should be sitting next to him, not me. You should be having his babies. You should run this place and organise teas and visit vicars and understand horses and know how to automatically give commands. You can make him happy, and I want him to be happy more than I want anything else.

Laura's greatest friend at Chartley was Charles, the estate manager, and an old friend of Nick's. He'd been there at the beginning of their relationship and she could actually talk to him about things. After she left for America, Charles told her afterwards, Nick didn't sleep for weeks. They could hear him pacing up and down in his room at night. Nick's personal quarters on the top floor of the house hadn't been touched since the time of his grandfather. Now, they remained mostly unused again as Nick was either outside or in meetings. He spent as little time as possible there and only came back to sleep in his room, a tiny grey attic with sloping windows, as far away from the rest of the house as it was possible to be.

Charles was by now married to Nick's younger sister Lavinia, and, at the time, their bedroom was directly below Nick's. After a week, Lavinia had gone upstairs and banged on her brother's door.

'Shut up with your clomping around in the middle of the night when the rest of us are trying to sleep,' she'd yelled, unaware of the noise she was making, or indeed the fact that she'd been convicted of noise pollution twice during her hippy-boho-stallholder-with-a-Portobello-Road-flat years. 'You've woken the baby up! I'm going to murder you!'

When did Laura realise she'd made a mistake, leaving Nick? Was it her third night in San Francisco, when she was in a bar with her new colleagues? 'You're The Best Thing That Ever Happened to Me' by Gladys Knight came on the jukebox and she had to pretend she had something in her contact lens so they wouldn't see her crying. Or was it every morning when she walked past the ice-cream parlour and thought how much Nick would love it? Or every time she went into her local bookstore and saw some quirky non-fiction book about the history of maths or something that she knew he'd enjoy? Or was it the clothes store that had a polo shirt he'd look so cute in, or the hippy tourist shop selling dreamcatchers that she always wanted to tell him about, because they both hated wind chimes and dreamcatchers almost as much as they loathed fat chips?

Maybe Laura realised she'd been wrong to leave him after allowing herself to Google him and discovering that he was now going out with Lara Montagu, and that she'd been right all along. Lara, she learned, was also an Olympic-standard showjumper. She'd actually quite liked Lara, and that only made it worse, this feeling that it was the right thing for him. Already she missed Nick so much it physically hurt. Her chest would ache as she lay in bed at night trying not to think about him, listening to police sirens and the sound of the Chinese family in the flat above her arguing. After that, she didn't Google Nick again.

But this rage Laura felt at knowing he was with someone else, this passion she had for that dark-eyed, quiet, shy man whose hands were always warm and whose heart she had used to hear beating as she fell asleep on his chest wouldn't go away.

She started to feel quite mad. She'd sit in cafés working on her laptop, drinking coffee and listening to the rain on the pavements and the cosy, relaxed West Coast chatter. She'd see how at home everyone else felt while she didn't seem to fit in at all. She loved the people, the freedom, the pride everyone took in the city. She felt she could live there and be happy, but one thing was stopping her. As the months passed she realised that was never going to change.

Laura asked herself, Would she have left Nick if the job in the States hadn't come up? Maybe not. She only knew she had to see Nick again.

Picking up her old life again in England was easy enough. Her boss, Rachel, was on maternity leave, they needed someone to cover for her. Sadly, Paddy had finally split from his girlfriend and wanted to rent a flat again. And so one spring evening back in London, Laura gritted her teeth, had a large gulp of wine and dialled Nick's mobile. He answered immediately.

'Laura?'

And she'd said, 'Hi, Nick. I'm back.'

'Thank God,' he'd said, and his voice was hoarse. 'Can I see you? Is that why you're ringing?'

'Yes, please,' she'd said, holding back tears, because it was so damn lovely to hear him again. 'Can you come down here? Or shall I . . . I can get the last train—'

'I'm coming to you right now,' he'd said, and he'd put the phone down and jumped straight into a car. She'd had to leave him a message giving him her new address, and when he'd arrived later that night, on the quiet street in West Hampstead, she was waiting for him.

She heard the car and leaned out of the window to see him standing there in the road, looking up at her. His hands were clenched by his sides. When she buzzed him in and opened the door to her flat, she watched him taking the stairs three at a time, as her heart pounded in her chest and she told herself what she knew would always be true: *You will never love anyone the way you love him.*

The feel of his arms wrapping around her, his lips on her skin, his heart beating close to hers, and his voice saying, 'Jesus, Laura, I've missed you. Don't ever leave me again.'

'I won't,' she said. 'I won't,' and when she looked at him his eyes were swimming with tears, and she couldn't say anything else. Then the hours turned into days and the days to months, and they were so happy they'd found each other again.

The only problem was, of course, that nothing had really changed at all.

Rule Five:

Watch *Downton Abbey*.
You never know,
it may come in useful some day.

'Raise your chin, Laura. Turn towards me.' Laura twisted on the arm of the sofa, her back aching. 'That's it. Hold the book up a little. Now relax, look natural. Pretend it's just the two of you, a quiet evening in.'

'We always sit like this,' Nick said to the photographer. 'Just . . . you know, we come into the Red Drawing Room of an evening, and we plonk ourselves down on the eighteenth-century silk-covered sofa, facing away from each other, and I take up all the room while Laura perches on the arm, holding a book and just smiling. That's how we roll.'

'Yes sir,' said the photographer, snapping away, not even pretending to listen. 'Laura, love, a bit more from you.'

'Uh-uh,' said Laura, trying not to slide off the sofa.

'Right, some questions then,' said Jim Cutler, the beefy journalist who had been at the bookshop opening. He moved his recording device closer. 'Ready?'

Nick and Laura looked at each other. 'Ready,' Laura said.

'The bookshop's been open a week now, is that right? How's it going?'

'Really well,' Laura said. 'We've had a great first few days. Takings are good. We're just looking to finish the work at the back of the shop to complete the project, and we're nearly there. In our first week our customer numbers were—'

Jim Cutler cut in. 'So . . . Laura, do you help Nick with the running of the estate?'

They both laughed. Nick's hand stole towards hers. 'No way,' Laura said. 'I know my place.'

'That's not true,' said Nick. 'Remember the plans for the maze?' He looked at Jim. 'Laura thinks she's more of a city girl, and I'm trying to persuade her she's not.'

'One day I thought the sheep in the fields were a different flock, but it turned out they'd just had their wool cut off. Been shorn. Whatever.'

Nick bit his finger, trying not to laugh. 'Amazing technical lingo you've got there, Laura. Maybe you're right. What about the time you thought you saw a camel and it turned out to be a horse?'

'Shut up.' She turned to him, still perched on the arm of the sofa, her eyes sparkling. 'What about the time you cried when Pamela Stephenson came third in *Strictly*?'

'She was so musical, though,' Nick said, outraged. 'Her hold with James was the best I've ever seen.'

Jim Cutler was staring at them in surprise. 'OK.'

'Anyway,' said Laura, tearing her gaze away from Nick's and thinking she ought to change the subject, 'I like having something here I can help with. I'm not much good at anything else at Chartley, you see.'

'I don't think that's true,' Nick said, lowering his voice a little. 'I think you love this place as much as I do.'

There was a silence. She wished they were alone, properly alone, for once.

'So you argue, like all couples do, blah blah.' Jim was scribbling this down in his notebook.

'They'll love that. And Laura's Place, the book-shop, was it your idea?'

'Yes,' said Laura.

'So . . . you just said to your boyfriend, can you give me the money?'

'Er, no,' Laura said. 'I had to write business proposals for his family's Trust and for three other charities. I also had to apply for a loan from the bank and help from the council. It's taken two years to get this off the ground.'

'Sure, sure,' Jim said. He nodded in a dismissive way. 'What would you say, then, to those who accuse you of using your boyfriend's money and position to open this shop?'

'Well, I'd say yes, of course,' said Laura. She could feel herself getting annoyed. 'How else could I have done it?' She knew that didn't sound quite right and it wasn't what she meant. Nerves made her voice rise. 'It's a serious business proposal. We are still short of the fifty thousand pounds we need to get the whole thing going. But it's vital in this climate that we push ahead. One hundred and sixty libraries have been shut down in the last two years. A quarter of book-buying budgets have been slashed.'

She turned to Nick, hoping he'd back her up, but he was fiddling with his phone, and somehow this made her angrier. 'Hey.' She leaned down and pushed his hands.

Journalist Jim looked up, alert as a panther. Nick stuffed the phone into his pocket. 'Sorry. Crisis in the tea-room.'

Laura knew he was lying, in that split second.

'Great,' Jim said, scribbling some more. 'I'll get that all in, thanks Laura. So . . . wedding bells? When's the big day happening, hm?'

Laura was caught off-guard. 'For who?'

Jim Cutler laughed. '*For who*? For you, of course.' There was almost a note of scorn in his voice. 'Everyone wants to know. I was at the bookshop earlier and at least three people were wondering when you two are going to make an announcement.'

Because you asked them, that's why, Laura thought.

'I see,' Laura said. Nick was silent.

'Look guys, sorry. I have to ask this stuff, you know, it's my job. It's what sells papers. People love this kind of story, it's gold dust. It's what'll get you your money, too.' He didn't sound sorry at all. 'So what's the next step?'

Nick raised his hand. 'Look, Jim, we're not going to answer those kinds of questions.'

'Why? It's what people want to know.'

'Really? I can't imagine anyone's that interested.' Nick's voice was level, but Laura knew that tone. It meant, leave us alone. 'And it's no one else's business.'

'Is that all you've got to say about it to people who work on the estate and are wondering about their future? To our readers, who want you to be happy?'

Nick stood up. 'Yes. That's all I've got to say. Most couples don't have journalists and villagers breathing down their necks all the time. We're quite private. All in good time.' He cleared his throat. 'Hey, give us a break, Jim.'

He sat down on the sofa next to Laura and put his arm around her. She took his hand and squeezed it. 'Yeah,' she said, trying to show support. 'Just like Nick said.'

Jim watched them both, then asked calmly, 'D'you get on OK with your sister – Rose, is it?'

'Of course,' Nick said carefully, after a pause. Laura kept a straight face. 'She's a bit bossy, but I tell her that all the time. Why?'

Jim shrugged. 'Well, Lady Rose told me you've been saying you're desperate to have children. She said you're worried about the future and who'll inherit this place. She said . . . where is it?' He flipped through the pages of his notebook. 'Here it is.' He read slowly, stumbling over his shorthand. 'Yes. "Nick has told me he has to make some changes. He needs to work out what happens with Chartley. You've seen *Downton*, Jim . . . we have to have a male heir. Sexist but true, I suppose!" Blah, blah . . . Oh yeah.

'Then she says "There are problems with Laura. I mean, we all love her, but let's face it, she's not a country type. She's more interested in a children's bookshop than she'll ever be in running Chartley Hall. She's made that clear to Nick, that's why he offered to bankroll it in the first place. He'd do anything to make her stay. But, you know, he's been hinting to me about various things lately. I'm not sure how much longer he can put up with it."'

Jim looked up at Laura and Nick, then carried on. 'Er . . . yes, then Lady Rose says, "He says he'll have sorted it all out by the end of the year." Bit brutal.' He flipped the pages back. 'What do you have to say to that?'

Nick swallowed and Laura saw his fists clenching, unclenching, opening and closing. She sat up and smiled, pretending everything was OK. 'Like we said, that's our business. Sorry, Jim.'

Inside her heart was thumping so loudly

she was sure they must be able to hear it echoing around the room. The only other sound was the photographer's camera clicking away.

Rule Six:

Don't storm out after a row. You may say things you regret, and besides, servants hear everything.

'I didn't say any of that stuff,' Nick said the moment they were out of the room. 'I'll have a word with Rose. She really shouldn't—'

'Have more than a word with her. Tell her to back off, Nick. Tell her to go back to London and stop interfering in our lives.'

He paused and put his hand on a side table. 'All in good time, Laura.'

Laura didn't want to lose her temper, not here. 'Fine.' She carried on walking down the long corridor, not really knowing what to say. The afternoon sun shone on the family portraits, lighting up the figures under the centuries-old varnish. A glinting eye here on a wicked old Earl; a winking diamond on a lady's hand; a creamy shoulder, proudly turned towards the onlooker, with a hand outstretched: *Look at us. We are the Needhams*. Laura had been down this corridor a hundred times, but it had never seemed so crowded before.

'It's not fine.'

'She's obviously saying something you told her.' She cleared her throat. 'You tell her things you don't tell me.'

'Well, there's a reason for that,' Nick said evenly.

Suddenly the atmosphere was different. They stood facing each other, and after a moment Laura said, 'Listen, I should think about getting that train. I'll call Charles, he said he'd drive me.'

She walked down the corridor as the last of the visitors was being ushered out of the library. 'Thank you! Hope you've had a wonderful day! You too, madam. Oh,' the guide said, biting her lip. 'Good evening, my lord.'

Her eyes followed Laura, but Laura couldn't speak all of a sudden. She nodded politely and opened the secret door.

Nick didn't follow her. 'Evening, Cynthia, lovely to see you.'

'Lot of visitors today my lord, all saying how excited they are about the new bookshop.'

'We're all excited about it. Have you been in yet?'

'No, my lord. Maybe next week, when it's less crowded. Did you hear about Marian?'

Nick leaned towards Cynthia and smiled, his face relaxing. 'No, what? Did she win the award?'

'Oh yes, my lord. She was so pleased she did a jig. Frank was there. He said he's never seen anything like it, even the judges were . . .'

Cynthia had a daughter, didn't she? But she also had a dog, perhaps it was the dog? But hadn't her dog just died? Laura shut the door quietly behind her and walked up the stairs to Nick's room. A powerful desire to be back in London overcame her again, though she knew it was childish. She couldn't help it: she'd rather be padding round the flat on a Sunday night with her hair in a towel, eating Thai takeaway and chatting to Jo on the phone than here.

Laura stood still for a few moments, looking around her, and then began throwing her things into an overnight bag. She found her hands were shaking. *There are problems with Laura. I mean, we all love her, but let's face it, she's not a country type.* No, I'm bloody well not. She wanted to open the windows and scream at the departing visitors,

I'm from Harrow! I got a rosebud duvet set from Marks & Spencer for my tenth birthday! My mum collects coupons! I'm like you! Take me with you!

She had already finished packing when Nick came in.

'Sorry about that. Cynthia's daughter's dog just won a prize at the county fair and I'd promised I'd go and I couldn't because of today . . .'

Laura zipped up the bag. *Is this Marian? Dog or daughter?* she wanted to ask, but she couldn't. Before today she would have done; they'd have laughed, and Marian would have been added to their long list of little jokes that only they shared. Like shouting 'SWAN!' loudly every time they saw a swan (from the film *Hot Fuzz*). Or saying, 'She sells sea shells on the sea shore,' as fast as possible whenever they passed a Little Chef in the car.

'You're not going now,' Nick said. It was a statement, not a question.

'Yeah, I am. I'll catch the seven o'clock train. I can be back home by nine, I've got work to do.' She fiddled with the zip again, not knowing what to do next. 'I guess I'll see you soon.'

'Laura,' Nick put his hands on her shoulders and said softly, 'I mean it. You know I didn't

49

say that. I don't know what Rose is talking about. Don't you believe me?'

'I want to believe you,' she said in a small voice. 'The trouble is I don't. Why would Rose make all that stuff up? "It'll all be sorted out by the end of the year." What did she mean?'

Nick's face was still right in front of hers. She stared up into his dark eyes, willing him to say something, anything that would explain it. *I'm selling the house. I'm studying for an A Level in Clown Studies and I have to appear in pantomime for the whole of December as part of my coursework. We'll be engaged by then.* But she knew Nick, and what she loved most of all about him is that he always told the truth. He couldn't lie, he was incapable of it. The most he'd ever deceived her was when they'd first met.

Now she looked at him.

'Do you see me here with you at the end of the year? Us together?'

He paused, and in that tiny, fatal second she knew something was up.

'Yes, of course. I mean, I know we've had things to sort out, and that this is a strange time for us, but for God's sake Laura, yes of course.'

Laura could feel her heart thumping hard in her chest again. She swallowed. Was this it?

'Right. So, what do you think needs to happen, then? Do I need to go on a course to learn how to be a proper lady? A bit like your sisters?'

'Don't be childish.'

'I'm not being childish.' Laura's blood thundered in her ears. 'Nick, can't you see? This is all wrong. This isn't how we're supposed to be. We've let all these other things, all these people, tell us what to think and how to be.' She picked up the bag, bending over so he couldn't see the tears forming in her eyes, then straightened up, trying to sound calm. 'I thought things would be different when I came back fr . . . from the States. But the same old problems keep coming up again. The same . . . things.' She tried not to let her voice break. 'I should go. It's best if I – look, maybe I won't come down next week.'

'You can't just run out again, like you did last time,' Nick said, his eyes glittering with anger. 'You've got this damned shop now, that should keep you here if nothing else does.'

'I'm so glad you see it like that. As some kind of anchor to tie me here. Nick, I want to be here, but I . . . I don't know what's up with you lately.'

'I wish you'd just trust me.' He turned away.

Laura balled her hands into fists. 'How can

I trust you when you fiddle with your phone all the damn time and won't tell me what you're up to? When I don't know how you spend your days? When you go off and tell your sister you need to have a damned *son* but you don't think I'm the right person for the job.'

'I didn't—'

'Did you say that stuff to Rose?' she shouted. 'Did you?'

'It wasn't like that,' he said quietly. His voice was neutral. 'Can't you . . . understand?'

The evening sun fell into the room, bathing them in rosy light and long shadows. 'I don't recognise myself any more when I'm down here. It's the same as always. Oh, Nick. I love – I love you. But we keep having this problem and we can't get past it. We have to change. Something has to change.'

'I don't want you to change.' Nick took a step towards her. 'Laura, I've never asked that. I want you to stay the same. The person I fell in love with.' His face was an inch away from hers. 'I just wish you . . .' He put his hands on her cheeks. She could feel his breath.

'Wish I what?'

'Wanted it all more.' His hands dropped to his sides. 'This.'

She felt so sad then. 'I do want it.' Laura

picked up her bag again and slung it over her shoulder. 'But maybe I'm not the right person for the job.' Her voice was small. She thought she would cry and she mustn't cry; she had to let him see she wasn't a child throwing a tantrum, that this was important to her. She touched his arm. 'Let's just cool off and speak during the week.'

'Laura,' he began, then stopped. 'Fine. You're right.'

Charles drove her to the station. In the golden summer dusk the Norfolk countryside was peaceful. A rabbit scuttled across the road, swallows darted in and out of the hedgerows. As they drove up to the station forecourt, Charles turned the engine off and said, 'It's a great success, your shop, Laura.'

She turned to him with tears in her eyes. 'Thank you, dear Charles.' She leaned over and kissed his cheek.

'What was that for?' Charles said, amused.

'Nothing.' For never making me feel like an outsider, she wanted to add, but she was sick of herself by now, and bitterly regretting not having parted from Nick on a warmer note. Already she was sure they had both overreacted, her especially. She was tired, the run-up to the opening of the shop had taken it out of her. They'd both said too much.

Laura climbed onto the near-empty train and stared out of the window. She watched as they pulled away, rolling through the flat, empty Fens, the sky above vast and flecked now with red. Red sky at night, shepherd's delight. She knew that, she thought, with a little chuckle. Perhaps she could turn into the kind of girl Nick seemed to need, an all-purpose country wife, well bred, good with kids, animals, old ladies, extremes of weather, expensive plates and vast houses?

Her phone buzzed and she leapt for it, realising how eager she was to hear from him, how little she wanted it to end like this.

Coming to London. Laura doesn't know. Can we meet? I need to see you. Can't stop thinking about what you said. I've made a big mistake. Want you to move to Chartley with me ASAP now. All my love, Nick x

Rule Seven:

If it goes wrong, just tell yourself it was all ridiculous anyway and it's nice to be back in the real world.

'Paddy, it's a terrible idea.' Laura took another sip of coffee and shovelled some more muesli into her mouth.

'It's not.' Her flatmate put his hands on his hips. 'I'm going to walk down the stairs casually, right? Then I'll sort of crumple to the ground and kick her door with my foot, and make an "Ahhh! Oww!" sound. Kirsty will come running to the door, she'll see me there and she'll invite me in and then . . .' he rubbed his hands together. 'Bingo. Bin. Go.'

Laura sighed. She'd known Paddy for nearly all her life and lived with him on and off for five years or more. She had also lived with Paddy through the Becky years, and she still couldn't understand why his lovely girlfriend, who'd seemed perfect for him, had finished with him. Then sometimes she'd come into the kitchen and see him in his pants, squatting earnestly in front of the washing machine, waiting for his one pair of trousers to finish drying, and she'd understand why a bit more.

She speared a piece of toast with her fork and began slathering it with Marmite. She was eating a lot of Marmite at the moment. 'Paddy! You always do this, stop it! This is why girls keep telling you to curl up and – what was it that girl said to you last week?'

'"Curl up and die, pube-head." Why?' Paddy looked surprised. 'What do you mean?'

'You're way too full-on! Stop being weird. She's said no to you three times. I don't understand how you think throwing yourself down the stairs is going to change anything. Other than land you in hospital with a broken leg.' She looked at her watch. 'I'm going to be late.'

'Too full-on? I don't think so. I say if you like someone, give yourself up to them. Just be really open about it.'

'But look where that's got you, Pads.'

'You've got to be prepared, not scared. That's my motto.' Paddy put his mug on the draining board and looked round the small, scruffy kitchen. 'Have you seen my other sock? It's orange. So, is it work work today, or posh people work?'

Laura frowned and stood up. 'Hey, they're both work. Leave it.' She opened the fridge. 'I'll get more milk.'

'I know.' Paddy followed her into the hallway. 'But you know what I mean.'

'Work work,' Laura said, trying to make a mental shopping list. Without really thinking she added, 'The bookshop's all off for the moment.'

'What?' Paddy froze in the middle of plucking his other orange sock from behind a dead rosemary plant on the hall shelf. 'It's all *off*?'

Laura flushed and bit her lip. 'I didn't mean that. I only mean Casey wants to work there full time for the summer because her kids are away with their dad, and she's trained up Brian, too – he's the vicar's husband.'

Paddy chuckled with relief. 'Wow. It's another world up there. Where's the Belgian detective and the butler in the library with the drainpipe? And the society beauty with a dark secret?'

Laura ignored him. 'It's good for Casey if I leave her to get on with it a bit, find her feet. That's what I mean by it's all off. I . . . I don't have to go there for a couple of weeks. Anyway.'

She sifted through the bowl of crap on the shelf. Spare change, a horrible troll doll with fluffy pink hair, a ChapStick, two cracked Oyster cards, a couple of boiled sweets in foil wrappers (Nick always picked them up for her because she often got blocked ears and sucking on sweets helped). Laura paused, staring at the crinkling foil wrappers. They'd taken them up at a service station on the way to Jo's baby's christening.

She sells sea shells on the sea shore. She opened the door, but Paddy shut it.

'Hang on. You've been like this ever since you got back on Sunday,' he said. 'What's up, hmm?'

'Nothing!'

'How was that interview with the journalist – you were worried about it. Go OK?' Paddy narrowed his eyes.

'God, Paddy. Everything's fine.'

'Uh-oh. Trouble in paradise?' Paddy leaned against the door. 'Laura. I've known you since you were three, and don't forget I've known you at your most insane. When you were so obsessed with . . . what was that clarinet teacher called?'

'Oboe. Mr Wallace.' Laura folded her arms. 'I'm going to be late.'

'OK, oboe. Well, you were so crazy obsessed with Mr Wallace you used to hide behind a car and watch him drive off, then try and run after him to follow him to his house. I was there. I saw it. I told you to get a life and did you listen to me? No. Or when you were so in denial about Gideon being gay that you bought him the cast album of *Hello, Dolly!* for his birthday and you were all, "It's so great we've got so many things in common, like musicals and shopping." And remember when you stayed in your room for three days after Dan dumped you, and only came out after that pigeon flew in and smashed up the window?'

'What's your point?' Laura tried to push him against the wall, but Paddy patted her arm and said in a mournful voice,

'Don't try and shut me out, man, OK? I know you better than you think, Laura. What's going on with you and Nick? You guys are great together. Don't—'

Laura shoved Paddy out of the way. 'Let me go,' she said roughly, surprised at the strength of her anger. 'It's none of your bloody business. Just get a life, Paddy. Worry about yourself, not me. I'm fine,' she added, and she ran down the stairs so he couldn't see her face.

Rule Eight:

Jane Austen heroines
never had to use buses.

Safely installed on the top deck of a bus, rumbling painfully slowly into town, Laura ignored her feelings of guilt and slid her phone out of her bag. She stared for the millionth time at Nick's text, as if it might suddenly come to life and talk to her. Who was it for? *Can we meet? I need to see you.*

She'd left Chartley three days ago and she hadn't replied to the text. At first she'd been too angry, then she hadn't known what to say. But she'd had enough of being passive. She rang him. If it was going to end, it had to happen some time, didn't it?

'This is Nick. Please leave a message.'

'Hi. It's me. Give me a call, can you? We should talk. I want to . . . talk. OK. OK, bye.' She threw the phone back into her bag with a cry of frustration. It was Nick – *Nick* – and what the hell had happened to them that she couldn't even leave him a normal message asking him to call her?

'Please don't let it be true,' she whispered under her breath.

But she could see, with a kind of weary acceptance, that it probably was. He was having an affair, and when you thought about it, with everything that had been going on lately, it made sense.

The bus juddered to a halt on the Edgware Road and Laura's knees knocked against the seat in front. It was a hot day, especially hot on the top deck, and it wasn't even nine o'clock. Her fellow commuters sat in silence, music blaring from their headphones. Already she felt sweaty and grimy, and a feeling of delayed anger, of queasiness that hadn't left her since Sunday began to bubble within her.

She looked at her phone. She tried to read, but couldn't concentrate. She looked at her phone again. The bus remained static. A trickle of sweat ran down her armpit into her waistband.

After a few minutes, Laura couldn't stand it any longer. She went downstairs, into the fleshy pack of commuters. The next stop was less than ten metres away. She stood next to a slim, small man with a backpack who was humming under his breath.

'Could you open the door please?' someone asked the driver. He ignored them.

Someone else said, 'Please, can you just let us out? We're only a few yards from the stop.'

Nothing. Laura could feel another trail of sweat sliding between her shoulder blades. *Let us out*, she wanted to scream. Her head, which was already aching, started to pound. Her inner London rage began to bubble. *Give us a break. We're ten metres away!*

The passengers hummed and harred, muttering to themselves, but no one did anything. Laura crossed her arms, trying to stay calm. She didn't feel calm. She had a meeting at nine thirty.

Someone started ringing the bell, a constant *ding ding ding* that wormed into Laura's skull. The driver ignored it. A lairy-looking thickset man yelled at no one,

'He can't let us out. It's not his job. Shut it.'

'It's ten metres away!' a woman shouted, dangerously close to meltdown. 'He's being a total prick!'

'Uh-oh,' said the humming man next to Laura

in a sing-song voice. 'Uh-oh! Here we go!'

Laura suddenly lost it. 'This is ridiculous. Excuse me,' she said, barging her way towards the exit. She reached up and pressed a red button above the doors with a tiny sign next to it which said, 'FOR EMERGENCY USE ONLY'.

'Hey! That's illegal,' yelled the bus driver, suddenly awake. 'You're in breach! Close that door.'

With a Superman-like heaving sound, Laura shoved open the doors, then jumped off the bus and motioned for the other passengers to follow her. 'Follow me please,' she hissed, like Maria von Trapp in *The Sound of Music,* guiding the children away from the Nazis.

Some looked horrified, as if she'd just committed murder. Others jumped off with her as the driver jammed the doors shut again, shouting, 'Back on the bus! Everybody, *back on the bus!*'

'No!' shouted Laura, unneccessarily loudly. 'I will not get back on your damn bus!'

The other rebel passengers had dispersed, the doors had closed and the bus was now, miraculously, moving on. Laura realised she was just a crazy person standing alone on a pavement yelling. She turned on her heel and slipped off down a backstreet, too embarrassed to walk past the driver. Though she would never admit it to anyone else, sometimes she hated London.

A light breeze soothed her nerves as Laura walked briskly through the quiet, pretty streets of Marylebone, chewing her lip. Laura's granny, Mary, who had died a few years ago, had lived in a tiny flat off Baker Street and coming back this way always made Laura think of her. Mary wasn't like a normal granny. She drove too fast, liked gin and played poker. She was wise and kind, and Laura had loved her, almost as much as her parents. Walking around here again made her realise how much her life had changed, and at the same time how little. She wondered what Mary would say to her if she were around now. She wished she could just turn the corner, trot up the steps of the apartment building and find her grandmother there, reading a book and half-watching the racing.

She was so busy remembering her grandmother Laura didn't notice that she'd turned into Manchester Square, where Nick's family had a flat. The Needhams had once owned a whole house just round the corner from Claridge's in Grosvenor Square, a huge, soulless place draped in greying net curtains and seventies silk wallpaper, but Nick had sold it to settle some of the estate's debts and bought this instead, though he rarely used it, preferring to stay with her when he was in London instead. It had three bedrooms, a marble staircase, beautiful parquet flooring and a lovely roof terrace and was by far the nicest flat Laura had ever seen in her life, but she didn't like staying there. Somehow it seemed fake, when her own homely, chaotic flat was a just couple of miles away.

She stood at the corner of the square and checked her watch. It was after nine and she was now officially going to be late for her meeting.

In her twenties she'd been prone to shuffling into work with bird's nest hair and (only once) a pair of the previous day's knickers caught up in her tights, but Laura was older and, she hoped, a little bit wiser now. Her dad had once told her that he'd never had a sick day in his life, and that had made her sit up. George Foster had left school at sixteen to help his dad, who was a grocer. He'd gone to night school, become an IT engineer and worked every day he could to provide for his family. Now she was older, Laura realised that money had been tight in their house while she was growing up. But her mum and dad had never let Laura or her brother know or made them feel as if they were lacking anything that really mattered.

And what did her dad have to show for all those years of hard work? Virtually nothing. The pension fund he'd paid into all his life had collapsed the previous year, when the owners fled to Cyprus and the money vanished. George had said it was a bit like a magic trick, only a really rubbish one. Laura thought he should have been angrier than that. *She* was angry about it, about the way it always seemed to be normal people who lost out and rich people, getting away with it again.

Her parents had been down the week before the shop opened. They were still a little in awe of Chartley Hall and everything to do with Nick's world, though not Nick himself, whom she knew – she couldn't help but know – they adored. Nick and Laura, and Laura's dad in particular, loved Robert Dyas, the hardware shop on the high street that sold absolutely everything you needed – and a lot of stuff you didn't realise you needed. A trip to Harrow was never complete without a visit to Robert Dyas. Laura often felt Nick would have been much happier as a handyman or a farmer than a Marquis, cutting ribbons and wearing suits, standing with his hands behind his back, talking to strangers. He could spend hours in a hardware shop with Laura's dad, comparing mulch, mouse poison, barbecue covers and patio umbrellas with crank handles. All the things he couldn't buy for Chartley, where there was a gardener and a system for everything – and that didn't involve discounted garden hoses or instant-lighting charcoal at ten pounds for two packs.

Laura stared up at Nick's flat, on the other side of the square. She noticed the clematis growing up the side of the building was a little out of control. She wondered if she should order Nick a set of garden equipment from Robert Dyas for the flat's miniscule balcony as a peace-making gift, then she remembered the text again. Oh, no. As she gazed up at the french windows, something moved behind the glass and she jumped. She saw someone peering out, and then the curtains were closed, hurriedly.

Laura stood, frozen to the spot, and after a minute or two the front door opened and Nick stood on the doorstep, holding the door open as he'd done the other day for her, with a smile on his face. Then Lara Montagu emerged, and Nick followed her down the front steps and put his arm around her.

Rule Nine:

Real life isn't like the movies. Real life sucks.

Lara Montagu sidestepped a scooter and crossed the road. Her long blonde hair glimmered like a sheet of golden silk, a big Mulberry satchel was slung across her slim frame. By her side walked Nick, his hands in his jeans' pockets. He was relaxed and smiling. In fact, he looked happier than Laura had seen him for weeks.

Despite everything, Laura was completely taken by surprise. She stood rooted to the spot, and only as they came towards her at the other end of the square did she realise she had to hide. She scuttled up the steps and hid in one of the shadowy porches.

As the pair drew closer she could hear Nick say, 'Are you sure you want to do this?'

Laura peered out slowly, as Lara took Nick's hand and kissed it. 'Yes, of course, you idiot.

I've been waiting for you to realise what a mistake you made last time—'

'It wasn't a mistake. It just wasn't the right time for us,' Nick said.

'And it is now, you mean?'

Lara Montagu laughed. She looked so glad to be with him, that was the thing. Laura could almost have been happy for her.

As they passed by, Laura turned away slowly, rummaging in her bag as if looking for her keys, in case they should look up and see a strange girl on a neighbour's doorstep. But as she slowly twisted back to watch them, she realised she might as well have been naked and playing the bongos for all they cared. They were totally absorbed in each other.

Nick said, 'Lara, you do realise what you're taking on, don't you? The whole thing?'

Lara laughed. 'Absolutely. She wasn't right for you, Nick darling. She wasn't.' She kissed his hand again as they walked away, their voices growing fainter. 'At last! You're all mine. I can't wait to tell everyone.'

Laura stood motionless in the dark, grimy porch until she was sure they'd disappeared. For a moment she didn't know what to do.

She wondered if she should go home.

Then she thought of her dad. She brushed something away from her cheek, squared her shoulders and walked down the steps, in the opposite direction to Nick and Lara.

'Fine. It's going to be fine,' she whispered.

She walked and walked, down towards the river and the office. She didn't cry, she just kept on walking. When she got to work, she swiped her pass across the gate and waited for the lifts. They were always slow and so, as she always did, she took out her phone as something to fiddle with.

The photo of Nick on her phone screen was what set her off in the end, not the words of the text or what she'd heard Lara say. It was his face in the photo, arms waving madly at her on a boat in one of the channels that ran to the Norfolk coast. Nick, with his trousers rolled up, hair ruffled, holding on to a crab. Or rather the crab, pincers sunk into his finger, holding onto him.

She remembered that day last summer. They had taken the boat out, spread a picnic rug on the beach, far away from anyone else at the edge of the wild shore, and they had made love in the sand. Afterwards, as she lay with her head on his chest, hearing his heart beating,

Laura had felt completely at peace. She knew he was her home. She felt perhaps she'd never been closer to him than at that moment, their clothes ruffled, the warm sun beating down, the quiet distant crash of the sea. They ate cold ham with lots of mustard and thick bread, coleslaw and bottles of Coke. On the journey back they didn't really speak, just sat quietly next to each other. And when the little boat reached the tiny harbour, the tinkling sound of the masts in the wind sounded like the delicate chimes of a music box. It felt as though they had been in a dream and were only just waking up.

She knew now that it was true. It *had* all been a dream. And as she stared at the photo in the soulless glass lobby of her office, tears rolled down her cheeks.

Rule Ten:

If it's really all over, at least you've learned something about . . . history, stately homes and antiques, right?

The day only seemed to get worse. Rachel, Laura's boss, was on maternity leave again and Laura and her colleague Nasrin were in charge. Since Nasrin preferred quizzes in *Pick Me Up!* and chats about what was happening with the Kardashians to actual work, the morning was trying. The afternoon was even more so, as Rachel rang, off her head from lack of sleep and in floods of tears about her husband Marcus and how useless he was being with the new baby. Since Laura had set them up in the first place, she felt one hundred per cent responsible, especially when Rachel finished by sobbing, 'I honestly wish I'd never met him, Laura!'

Then Casey called from Laura's Place, saying the carpet fitters still hadn't finished the trim and Mrs Wilson had tripped on the loose carpet at the back and twisted her ankle. Also, half the books they'd ordered hadn't arrived from the wholesalers and the computer programme Laura had set up wasn't working.

'I'm trying my best,' she said to Laura rather helplessly, 'but I don't think I'm experienced enough to deal with a lot of it. Are you coming up at the weekend?'

Laura said slowly, 'I wasn't going to. But I can if you need me. Do you want me to come up?'

Casey sounded relieved. 'Yes. Yes I really do. Sorry.'

'It's fine, no problem.'

'Great. We've made gingerbread and lemonade, like in the Maisy books,' Casey added shyly. 'It's looking lovely here.'

Laura couldn't help wishing she was there, the cool country breeze wafting in from the street, children playing in the garden and drinking lemonade.

'I'll be up before lunch on Saturday,' she said. 'I'll go over everything and then it'll all be fine.' Her throat tightened at the thought of this lovely place she'd helped make, and which she might never see again after the weekend.

'There's one other thing. Lady Rose was in here yesterday,' Casey said, 'with some business bloke. She said he was something to do with some foundation or other? She had a good look round and was asking all the children questions and the like. She told Brian she didn't think he should be working with children too. He's a bit upset about it. Said he was too old and he wouldn't understand what they need.'

Laura stabbed her pen gently onto her notepad. 'She said what?'

'Lady Rose asked to see the accounts too. I said there wasn't much point as we've only been open ten days, but she said you'd told her it was OK. Something to do with the extra funding for the children's centre. I think that's why she'd brought this guy with her. He was wearing a suit and he kept taking notes. She said—' Casey stopped. 'Sorry, Laura. Should I not have let her?'

'It's fine.' Laura tried to sound unruffled. 'Don't worry about it. If she comes back, tell her to give me a call, will you?'

'I will.'

'Is Brian alright?'

'Oh he's fine. I told him not to get himself in a flap about it, you'd sort it out. So we'll see you Saturday? Do hope you're pleased with what we've done Laura.'

Laura cleared her throat. 'I'm sure I will be. Thanks, Casey.'

As she put the phone down, she wondered, for the millionth time since Sunday, why Nick hadn't noticed he'd sent the text to her and not Lara. It was easy to explain in part. Nick hated mobiles and could barely be persuaded to have one. His was a very big old Nokia, with typeface like a calculator. It sent texts and made calls and that was it. He stored numbers by first names, and she knew Lara and Laura would be right next to each other. He obviously hadn't noticed that he'd revealed he was cheating to his own girlfriend. Or maybe he had and he just didn't care.

Laura tried to rein in her overactive imagination, but that evening, going home on another slow, crowded bus, she realised that if they split up, she wouldn't be involved with the shop any more, presumably. Or would she? She wondered how soon Nick would propose to Lara, and with the clarity of the heartbroken she bet herself it would be within the year. She understood it now. All that talk to Rose had been true: he wanted to get married, just not to her. And when they were married, the new Lady Ranelagh wouldn't want Laura popping up in the village saying, 'Don't mind me! I'm just his bitter ex-girlfriend who didn't quite make the cut! Carry on. Would you like to buy a copy of *The Gruffalo* for your adorable children?'

She stopped off at the corner shop and bought some beers and, when she reached the flat, rang the bell three times before letting herself in. This was the house code for 'I'm back and I need some company'. Laura had instituted it as a response to Paddy's assumption that the moment she got back from work she'd like nothing more than Paddy leaping around her telling her about his day and singing Elbow songs loudly while she tried to have a cup of tea and generally wind down.

He appeared in the kitchen, worn green shirt stained with biro, and looked at her warily.

'Hello there.'

'Look, I'm sorry for being such a cow today,' Laura said. She put the six-pack of bottles down on the kitchen table with a thud. 'Nick is cheating on me. He texted me instead of some other girl by mistake, and today I walked past his place in the centre of town and he was coming out of the flat with an ex of his called Lara and I heard them talking. So everything's crap, basically.' She cracked open one of the bottles with her hand and the top flew up into the air. 'Cheers.'

Paddy looked at her, astounded. 'Jesus, Laura.'

'Yeah.' She drank deeply.

'Are you sure? I mean, I don't *not* believe you, but Nick, man! Nick! He's mad about you. He loves you like . . . well, I've never seen anyone like that. He looks at you like you're saving him from drowning.'

Laura glanced away, so he couldn't see the tears that sprang into her eyes. 'That's lovely, Pads.' She handed him a beer. 'I think he used to, maybe. Not any more.'

'No, no,' Paddy said. 'Laura, I'm sure you've got this wrong. Let me see the text.'

Laura showed him the phone and he read it. Then he took a long swig of beer. 'Right. I see what you mean.'

She gave a weak grin. 'Thanks, man. I was hoping you'd tell me I was mad.'

As Laura was holding the phone, it started to ring.

'It's him!' Paddy screamed. They looked at each other in total panic. Paddy even glanced anxiously out of the window, as if Nick might be standing outside.

Laura smiled then – it was so silly – and answered the phone.

'Hi.'

'Hi. Laura. How are you?'

'I'm fine. OK. Are you in London?' she said, though she knew the answer.

There was a silence. 'No. Why? I'm with Charles. We're just going over a few things. Can you talk?'

'Sure, I can talk.'

Paddy began nervously banging cupboards, looking for some crisps.

'Where are you?'

'I'm in the kitchen with Paddy. Why?'

'Oh. Right. This is – well, can you go some-where more private? There's something we really need to discuss.'

Was he going to dump her over the phone? He wouldn't do that, would he?

'I'm fine. I said I can talk, I didn't say for long. What's up?'

She could hear him sigh. 'OK. I wondered if you were coming up this weekend? I really think we need to sit down and go over some . . . things.'

She managed to say, 'I agree.'

'You do?'

'Yes, the shop especially.'

'That's it.' He sounded relieved.

'Rose was there yesterday, looking round with

78

someone. She asked to see the accounts. Do you know anything about it?'

'No. Was it to do with the funding? That might be why.'

'She's not on the board of the Needham Trust, Nick. Why does she need to go poking round in my business?'

'I suppose she thinks—' He stopped abruptly. 'I don't know.'

'What were you going to say?'

'Nothing.'

She didn't care how ugly or angry her voice sounded. She wanted him to side with his family and reject her, to make this easier. 'Go on. Tell me. You think she thinks it is her business.'

'No.'

'Tell her to back off! She upset Casey. She told Brian he was too old to be working with children – I mean, what does that *mean*? Why can't she just go back to her life and stop telling us how to run things?'

There was a pause. 'I thought you didn't care about how we run the estate,' he said.

Laura faltered. 'I do when it's my shop and my arse on the line.'

'Things have never been so tough here. She . . . she's just trying to help.'

'Things are tough for everyone, Nick.'

Nick's voice was steely. 'Five hundred people work here in the summer, Laura. I'm the biggest employer in the area. You don't think I'm aware of that? Rose will calm down, but not at the moment. Spare me your – oh, never mind.' He gave a deep sigh. 'Look, please come down this weekend. I really do need to see you.'

Something about the way he said it was so final.

'OK,' she said. 'I'll come up on Saturday morning. I've said I'll be at the shop by lunchtime.'

'Saturday afternoon would be best. I have to help with the maze, we're trimming the hedge all day.'

'Are you serious?'

'I'm the only one who knows the way out.'

Ridiculous, crazy place. A ball of laughter that threatened to turn into a sob bubbled up inside her. 'Fine.'

'That's – that's great. Sure, just coming,' he called to someone else. 'I have to go,' he said. 'We've got some builders in – work upstairs that needs doing. I hope it's not too disruptive when you get here. If you can't find me, ask Mrs Simmons or Clive to show you—'

'Nick, I know what to do,' she said, aware that her voice was rising. Paddy stared at her, his eyes wide. 'See you then.' Laura put the phone down. She steadied her hand on the kitchen counter. 'It's totally phase two up there. Out with the old. Oh, Paddy.' She wiped a tear away from her cheek. 'It's happening, isn't it? I'm being pathetic. I just didn't think it'd be like this. I suppose I always thought . . . Well, I always thought we'd make it.'

'This is terrible,' said Paddy, in a hollow voice. 'Laura, I'm so sorry.'

Laura sat down at the table again and put her head in her hands. She stared at the patterns in the wood, the lines of the grain flowing under her fingers. This was it. It really was going to happen, and had she made it happen? The question was, would she try and fight him? Tell him they should give it another go?

It sounded ridiculous to even think it. She knew the answer.

Behind her, Paddy cleared his throat. 'Can I ask you something?'

'Sure.' She drank the rest of her beer.

'What you said about me, this morning. You said I was too full-on, too weird with girls, that I was too open with them.'

'That's not a question.' Laura blew her nose. 'I might find some wine.'

Paddy ignored this. 'Because, you know, I think if you love someone, or you think you might love them, you should definitely go for it first and worry about all the small, silly stuff that gets in the way later. And it might just sort itself out. So here's my question. Don't you? Think that?'

Laura looked in the fridge, bringing out a bottle of rosé. 'I know what you're getting at. This isn't small silly stuff, though, Paddy. It's everything.'

Paddy shook his head. 'But it's not, though. I think your trouble is you're still convinced you're this stupid girl who doesn't know her own mind. That you're the person you used to be, obsessed with some romantic dream.'

'Harsh,' Laura said, but she knew he was being serious. She bit her lip. 'Maybe.'

'What are you so afraid of?' Paddy pushed the beer towards her.

Laura shrugged. 'I can't say. It sounds stupid.'

'Come on. What is it?'

Laura found it hard to speak. She poured herself a glass of wine and drank most of it, all without looking at Paddy. Her heart was thumping in her mouth.

'Um – I suppose I don't want things to change.' She said it in a small voice. 'I don't want him to realise I'm not good enough for him. Nick needs someone so much, and I can't . . . I can't be that person. And I'm also scared I won't be good enough for him. That I'll let him down. And Dad, and Mum. So maybe it's easier to just be here with you, having a drink. Two drinks.'

Paddy thumped the table so hard Laura jumped. 'There! There you go!'

'Oh shut up,' Laura said.

'I mean it. I'm totally right. Laura, in ten years' time do you really think the ideal dream would be you and me sitting at this table drinking beers? 'Cos I think that'd be pretty tragic. Things change. It's scary because you don't recognise your new life for a bit, but then you get used to it. You think it's the house and the title and all of that, but it's not. And your mum and dad don't care, they're so proud of you already, can't you see that? Everyone is, you lunatic.' Paddy stood up, hugging himself. 'I'm bloody brilliant. It's not anyone else, it's you. You're the one creating all these obstacles. Because you don't recognise your life, and you're afraid of what you see, and you shouldn't be.'

'Where on earth did you get all that from?' Laura asked.

'*The Sound of Music* was on TV last Sunday. I've never seen it the whole way through.'

'You've never seen *The Sound of Music* the whole way through?!' Laura was astonished. 'I don't even know what to say to that, Paddy. How have you managed to know me thirty years and not seen it?'

'Dunno.' Paddy opened a packet of crisps. 'You go on about stuff too much sometimes. But anyway, that's what the old bird says to Maria before she starts singing "Climb Ev'ry Mountain". Think about it, Laura.'

Laura drank a large gulp of rosé. 'But you're forgetting something.'

'What?'

She smiled. 'Lara. Explain that one away.'

'Oh.' Paddy looked stumped. He sat back down again. 'Yeah. I forgot about her. Sorry.'

Rule Eleven:

Break-ups should never be conducted in a setting that could also be used in a BBC costume drama.

Laura fixed the bookshop's computer programme. She rang the wholesalers and yelled at them. She even got down on her knees and fitted the metal trim to the carpet. Not for nothing had George Foster instilled his children with a love of DIY and Robert Dyas. 'Where are you off to now, Laura?' Casey asked her when they'd finished going over the books.

'Up to the house,' Laura said.

Casey smiled shyly. 'Of course! You'll see his . . . Nick. Oh, that's lovely.'

You're what? Twenty-eight? And your husband left you and your two kids for a barmaid and your boyfriend's just dumped you, yet you're still excited about the girl having the Cinderella romance with the man with the title and the big house. Oh ladies, nothing's going to change while we're still obsessed with that.

Laura didn't say this, obviously. Instead, she nodded. 'Thanks a lot, Casey,' she said, patting her arm. 'You're doing an amazing job,' and she stumbled out before Casey saw the tears in her eyes. She didn't look back.

It was nearly a mile from the gates to Chartley Hall and, knowing she'd probably be driving straight back again afterwards, Laura decided to stretch her legs and walk up to the house. As she cut through the meadows and passed into the formal estate she breathed in. The scent from the wild roses and honeysuckle tangled in the hedgerows seemed to hang heavy in the air. Before her the dark green row of oak trees were totally still.

Chartley Hall shone golden in the waning sun. The windows glittered, the lead glass like diamonds catching the light. The rounded towers with their black iron weather vanes each seemed to tear a hole in the blue sky. Laura stopped and stared, as though seeing it for the first time, not the last. It was beautiful.

As she drew closer, she heard shouts from behind the house and the clank of builders' ladders. Then one of the vast library windows on the first floor was flung open. The glass caught the sun, glinting with fire. Laura stood still in surprise. You didn't just open the library windows. Its collection of books was priceless, the famous Hogarth Happy Marriage series of drawings was hung there and everything had to be kept at a certain temperature. But someone was swinging the window to and fro, like a maniac, catching the light. She had almost reached the great forecourt when the vast front door opened and Mrs Simmons, the new housekeeper, appeared. She welcomed Laura with a thin, nervous smile.

'Good evening, Laura, how nice to see you.'

'Evening, Mrs Simmons,' said Laura, mounting the steps. 'I wondered if—'

'His lordship particularly wanted me to look out for you, he said to send you straight over to the maze.'

Any faint hope she had of doing this in private was gone. 'Great. Thank you. I'll . . . great.' Laura strode off, feeling like a prisoner on her way to the Tower.

The maze had only recently been restored. It had once been one of the glories of the house and something of an early tourist attraction. Prime Ministers, Turkish Sultans, European nobles: they had all paid special visits to Chartley in the eighteenth and nineteenth centuries to see if they were clever enough to make their way to the centre and out again.

But after Nick's mother left, his father and the house fell into a Sleeping Beauty-like trance and the maze was, along with so much else, forgotten about. The box hedging had been allowed to rot and die, and when Laura first came to the house it was a large yellowing mulch, from which there was no sign of the original layout.

One night, not long after she had returned from America, she and Nick had been in the library, turning over old books together, with no sound but the two of them and the crackle of the log fire in the huge grate while an autumn storm raged outside. It had been a lovely if sometimes awkward day, getting to know and trust each other again. Suddenly, Laura had given a yell of exclamation, 'Look! Look, Nick! These are the old plans for the maze. This is it! It's bloody it!' He'd come over, the fire reflecting and flashing in his dark eyes. Glancing at the old yellowing papers she'd spread out on the wide table, he'd turned to her.

'God I love you, Laura Foster.' He'd caught her in his arms and twirled her round until they collapsed on the floor in a happy heap, and the plans nearly went up in flames.

When she reached the maze, she stopped at the entrance to the glossy box hedges and glanced into the dark green. It was quiet here, separated from the rest of the park by an oval of oak trees. Stone benches flanked the outside of the maze and a wood pigeon called lazily through the afternoon haze.

'Nick?' she called awkwardly. 'Nick, it's me. It's Laura.'

No answer. She turned round. A blackbird, hopping along the grass, eyed her curiously.

'Nick?' she yelled again.

Should she just go? She looked round again, not sure what to do. The setting sun hung over the bottom of the huge park like a giant, rose-gold ball.

'I'm inside,' came a distant voice. 'Come and find me.'

Laura hesitated.

'Who is that?' she called.

The voice laughed. 'Laura, it's me, you idiot. Who else would it be?'

Laura entered the maze. 'I don't know,' she said, listening carefully. Her heart was in her throat at the idea that he was so near and yet so distant from her. 'It might be . . . well, some

kind of homicidal maniac. Waiting with an axe.
You can't be too careful.'

'You're right.' His voice was nearer. She
turned the first corner, back on herself. 'If I was
a homicidal maniac with an axe, I'd definitely
spend hours making my way to the centre of
a maze then lie in wait for hapless visitors.
That's definitely how I'd ply my trade.'

Laura stopped. The spicy, grassy smell of the
box hedge hung over everything. At the end
of the passage were two turnings. An arrow had
been hung from the tree, and a sign, decorated
with bunting, said:

This way →

'It's cheating to have a maze where you point
out the route.' Laura kept following the arrows.
'Now I'm further away than I ever was.' There
was silence. 'Nick?'

But there was no answer. She put her hand
to her collarbone and breathed deeply, trying
not to feel panicked or cross. She walked on
slowly, following the curve of the circle almost
back to where she'd started.

Then she saw the next sign, festooned with
fairy lights.

Things may be tough sometimes,
Laura, but as long as you trust
me, I promise I'll never, ever let
you get lost. This way →

Laura frowned. 'Nick?' The path doubled back
again to the outermost circle of the maze. This
couldn't be right, could it? She read the sign
again, her heart pounding.

And suddenly she heard her grandmother
Mary's voice. She used to hear it all the time
in the year or so after she'd died, but not
recently. Not until now.

You have a great capacity to love, Laura. Use it.
Stop wasting it. Throw yourself into it and don't
be scared.

'Nick?'

She started walking again, more quickly this
time. The maze twisted to the left and then
to the right, but each turn had an arrow
showing her the way, and at the end was
another sign, covered in flowers, bunting and
fairy lights.

I will always love you, no matter
what happens. I will always look
after you, no matter what
happens. And I need you to look

after me, too. We need each
other.
I love you, Laura.
This way →

'Nick? *Nick?*'

'I'm here,' the voice called back. 'I'm right here.'

She walked to the end of the hedge, two more turns and she was at the centre, and there, waiting for her, was Nick. In one hand he held the last arrow. His face was white, his dark eyes fixed on her.

'Laura, you're here,' he said. 'You're finally here.'

Rule Twelve:

Never walk into a maze unless someone knows the way out.

Laura took it all in: the fairy lights strung along the hedges, two chairs decorated with wild flowers, and a table covered with clutter, material and bits of wood, as Nick came towards her.

'Lavinia and Charles helped me. Are you surprised?'

Laura's head was spinning. She stared up at him. 'Why have you brought me here, Nick? To make some kind of fool of me?'

He froze for a second, and his voice was quiet when he answered. 'I thought . . . it's supposed to be a surprise.'

Her voice was hard. 'A surprise for me? Or for Lara?'

He looked blank. 'For you, of course – what's Lara got to do with it?'

Laura pulled out her phone and took a deep breath. 'You sent me this text, didn't you?' He glanced at it. 'And then I saw you and Lara together. On the street outside your flat. You didn't see me.'

Nick sounded bewildered. 'Who are you? Someone out of *Midsomer Murders*? Why are you stealing my texts and following me around town?' He took her hand again. 'Laura, I know I've been an idiot the last couple of weeks. A total prick. I can't tell you how sorry I am.' He kissed her fingers, each in turn. 'The estate has been taking all my time lately, Rose has been winding me up and Charles is distracted because of the kids and my lunatic sister. I know I'm not patient enough sometimes, I don't put myself in your shoes. I've been trying to sort it all out so that I could—'

'Look, I know what's happening,' Laura interrupted, pulling her hands out of his grasp. 'I know you're having an affair with Lara, Nick. For God's sake, just admit it.' She waved her phone at him. 'Didn't you hear me? You sent me that text by mistake. And I saw the two of you talking, I . . . I saw you!' She felt her voice cracking. 'You said you wanted her to come to Chartley and she said, "I'm glad you've made up your mind, she wasn't right for you, everyone knows it."' Tears were falling down her cheeks and she gave a huge sob, the tension of this last week finally catching up with her. 'I s–s–stood there and heard you say it, don't deny it.'

He came towards her, concern etched on his face. 'My God. Oh my God, Laura. I'm so, so sorry.'

She stepped back. 'So it's true, isn't it? I mean, you're right. She's right. About me not being right for you.'

'Don't ever say that.' He shook his head, a pulse throbbing in his cheek. 'Laura, I meant Rose. I have to do something about her. I've been letting it go on for too long. I've been a chicken. That's what Lara's here for.'

'Pull the other one. It's got bells on.'

'She is! I've *hired* Lara, she's Head of Marketing!'

Laura said sarcastically, 'Head of *Marketing*? What are you, an ad agency?'

'How else is this place going to survive?' he said with a twisted half smile. 'That's what all the big houses have these days. Lions at Longleat, concerts at Woburn Abbey, the Mitfords and the grounds and the farm shop and everything else at Chatsworth.'

Laura watched him with her arms still crossed. 'But, Nick . . . you hate all of that. You hate the Costa Coffees going into stately homes, I've heard you say that so many times.'

'But it's still my future, our future, and I have to work out our plan for Chartley too. I'm not joking, it's do or die. You know, there's more, not less, interest in places like these every day, maybe it's the *Downton* effect. And Laura, I love the house. I don't want us to lose it. I'm sorry. I wish it wasn't like this, but it is. It's part of me.'

'Oh, Nick.' She stared at him. 'Of course it is. I know that.'

'There's nothing round here for young people, no jobs, no nothing. Lara's going to redo the stables and start a proper restaurant, with everything grown on the estate. We're going to run a youth programme, a bit like Jamie Oliver's Fifteen foundation, to train up people who want to get into catering and gardening. I'll run it. There's going to be a big farm shop, we're building affordable housing out towards the village, and they're filming a new Keira Knightley movie here next year. Lara says that'll take visitor numbers right up.'

He grabbed her hands. 'Listen to me. She's going to take on a lot of the responsibility of the estate, we're going to plough more than ever back into the community, and, well, I didn't tell you because I've been planning all this so I could tell you when . . .' He was pale. 'Laura, for God's sake! You seriously thought I'd cheat on you?'

'I'm sorry, I . . .' She stopped. '. . . I believed it. I've been an idiot.'

He pressed her hands to his chest. 'How on earth have we ended up like this?'

'It's my fault,' Laura began, and then she shook her head. 'It's partly my fault.'

'This was supposed to all be a wonderful surprise, saving the best bit till last. The funding's in place for your centre.'

Her eyes lit up. 'Seriously?'

'Absolutely. Lara sorted that out, too. She's persuaded some big bank to donate the rest. Guilt money. She was there the other day at the opening, I was terrified you'd see and guess what was going on.'

'I saw her,' Laura said casually.

'And that's not all. Rose is going to work for a charitable trust in London, she got the job through that bloke she dragged to the bookshop. He's the head of some government agency.'

'Typical.'

'Well, to be fair, she'll be good at it,' Nick said, ever loyal.

Laura swallowed down an unkind remark and said, 'Rose would have done a good job with this place. I feel sorry for her.'

'I don't,' said Nick. 'She's absolutely fine. Skin as thick as a rhino's.'

'God.' Laura pressed her hands to her flushed cheeks. 'I've got this all so wrong. I mean, wow! Really wrong. So, um, when does Lara move down here?'

'She's here already. She has a place by the sea.'

'Oh, right.'

'She's really nice, Laura. We're stabling her horses. It's all set, she's really excited about it. She was brilliant today. She was the one opening the library window up at the house – that was the signal that you were on your way. It flashes in the afternoon sun.'

'I . . .' Laura pushed each forefinger into her temple. 'Are you sure?'

'Of course I'm sure. Her husband's coming over tonight to help – well, you'll see later. We've got a bit of a celebration planned. I hope.'

'Her *husband*?'

'She's been married for three years. I was best man at the wedding,' Nick said.

'But the newspapers said you went out with her when I was in the States . . .' Laura put her hands over her face and made a noise, something between a sob, a laugh and a moan.

'The newspapers! You read it in a newspaper and you don't even ask me if it's true or not? I've never been out with her. I kissed her when we were ten, does that count?'

'Oh my word.'

'Oh my word indeed. Listen.' Gently, he pulled her hands away from her face and stared into her eyes. They were both still, the afternoon sun bathing them in golden light.

'Listen to me, Laura. I wrote those signs because I wanted you to come and find me here. Because I wanted to tell you I understand a relationship is like a maze. You just have to find your way through.' Nick stopped and took a deep breath. 'I meant what I said when I wrote it. As long as you trust me, I promise you'll never get lost. Ever, Laura. This is my home. It's where I live. I love you. I'll always love you. I don't want you to go back to London. I want you to stay here and make it your home too.'

As she moved towards him, Nick dropped to his knees and stared up at her, his brown eyes solemn.

'Laura Foster, will you marry me?'

Laura fell to her knees, too. She stared at him, biting her lip, and closed her eyes.

'Oh, Nick,' she whispered. 'I want to . . . so much.'

He looked at her and she looked at him, and the two of them started laughing. He took her hand in his and kissed it. 'Listen, my darling,' he said softly. 'This is how it'll work. I'll have my job – running the estate, kissing babies, all that lot. You'll have your job – running Laura's Place, the visitors' centre at the back, the reading programmes and all of that. And we'll come home in the evenings to Chartley. The builders have started work already. There's going to be a separate door installed and we're opening up the south staircase just for us, with soundproofing so no one can hear us. We'll have our own kitchen, sitting room, everything. We'll choose all the wallpaper and curtains and everything together. Or you can choose them yourself. I want you to feel like it's your home. And this.' He reached up and took something off the table, pushing the fabric samples aside, sending them fluttering to the floor. 'Here, Laura.'

It was a small brass plaque, with holes all ready to nail into the wall.

This is Nick and Laura's Place
Press bell and wait for admittance

'This is going on our front door, you see? At the bottom of the stairs. We'll come home, unlock our own front door and hang our coats up on our own coat hooks.'

'Right. Can we have my coat rack that Granny gave me? The one with owls on it?'

'I hate the way those owls stare at me like they're going to nibble my coat. But . . . OK!' They smiled at each other. 'Wow. If that's a dealbreaker, then, yup. We'll kick our shoes off, have a glass of wine. We'll laugh about the funny things that happened during our day. You know, some kid was sick on a pile of books or someone chopped his finger off in a threshing machine, that kind of thing . . .'

'That doesn't sound very mellow,' Laura interrupted. 'I'm out.'

He slid his hands around her waist and pulled her towards him. 'Then we'll have some dinner in our own kitchen, and we'll sit in our own sitting room, and we'll read or watch more boxsets about horrible murders or something, and then we'll go to bed and sleep and – whatever.' He bent his head to look at her, and she raised hers to meet him and they kissed.

'There'll be no one arriving in the middle of the night to tell you about a silage crisis?'

'No,' he said, kissing her back, his lips warm and smooth. She felt as though she were swallowing caramel, sweetness ran through her, lighting her up.

'No sisters storming in demanding to have some painting removed to their house in London or some cash for their hypno-birthing course?'

'Definitely no, and I'm sorry again about that.'

'Just us two?'

'Just us two,' he said. 'And whoever else comes along.'

'That sounds OK to me,' she said. He kissed her again and moved so his arms were holding her tightly, so she could feel the muscles under his skin move as she clung to him, tears running down her cheeks.

As if reading her mind, Nick said, 'I thought I was losing you. I thought you realised you'd made a mistake in coming back and I . . . I didn't know how to make you believe it wasn't a mistake.' His voice was hoarse. 'Dammit, Laura, I've screwed everything up. I wanted to tell you about Lara today, as part of the whole romantic proposal thing. I didn't realise it'd . . .' His arms tightened around her, his breath warm on her neck. 'Oh my darling. I've been so stupid. I forgot the most important thing of all.' He kissed her forehead.

'What's that?'

'That we work together. We just do. And I can't imagine my life without you.'

He stepped back and, still holding her hand in his, fumbled in his pocket. 'Hey, you haven't actually answered my question. Will you marry me?' he said again, taking out a ring.

It was gold, with a diamond and sapphire twisted together. Laura gasped. 'That's Granny's ring,' she said. 'How did you . . . ?'

'I was actually down in London this week to see your dad,' Nick said. He smiled. 'Not to conduct a secret affair.'

Laura shook her head, trying not to laugh, it was such an important moment. 'You went to see Mum and Dad?'

'I had lunch with them. I helped your mum with the garden, then your dad and I went to—'

She interrupted. 'You went to Robert Dyas, didn't you? With Dad? While I was sobbing and breaking my heart over you having an affair with some old blonde friend of yours.'

'Be fair. I didn't know you were sobbing and breaking your heart over me having an affair with some old blonde friend of mine. But yes, I went to Robert Dyas with your dad. We looked at leaf blowers. He bought me my own barbecue tongs. He said it was his way of welcoming me to the family.'

Her eyes were full of tears. 'I can't believe you went to Robert Dyas without me.'

'When we got back we told your mother, and she took me into the study and took this out of the bureau. She said, Laura, and I'm going to repeat it, "She'll have so much if she marries you, but I'd like the symbol of your engagement to be about where she came from, too. So that everyone knows how proud we are of her."'

Laura shook her head. 'Oh no, they shouldn't be proud. Not yet.'

He held her hand and stopped her. 'No. You have to be patient when you see your future for the first time, Laura. Sometimes you don't recognise it when you see it. Because it's going to be totally different from what you know and it seems frightening.'

'And what do you do when you find it?'

'You walk towards it,' he said, and he kissed her. 'You know that we've got each other and that's all that matters.' He slid the ring onto the tip of her finger. 'So? For the final time, what's your answer? I'm not going to ask you again, you know. Will you marry me?'

Laura laughed. 'This is my answer.' She kissed him. 'Yes, Nick. Yes, yes, yes.'

July 2013

From the *Norfolk Gazette*:

> Bookshop manager wanted, ideally with two years' experience, to cover present bookshop manager/owner's maternity leave. One year initial contract, but may be extended.
>
> Contact Laura Foster on laura@chartley.org

From the *Daily News*, July 2013:

> As the nation prepares for the arrival of a new heir to the throne, I hear from my sources in Norfolk that similar plans for change are afoot at the house of Ranelagh. You may remember that last year Nick Needham, aka the Marquis of Ranelagh, married his long-term so-called 'normal' girlfriend Laura Foster. I hear not only are bootees being knitted, but legal writs are being prepared. The Marquis and Marchioness have lodged an appeal at the High Court to ask that their child, whether it be boy or girl, have the right to inherit the 10,000-acre estate, essentially reversing centuries of tradition.

The Marquis is quoted as saying, 'I'm married to a remarkable woman, and she's expecting our first child. I can't wait to meet him or her, but when I do I want to be able to look them in the eye and say, "This is yours," no matter what their sex.'

The Marchioness added, 'If it's a boy, I want him to be just like his father. If it's a girl, I want her to grow up reading nothing but non-fiction and only watching TV documentaries with David Attenborough, current affairs programmes and medical dramas.'

It is understood that this is supposed to be a joke.

Announcement in *The Times*, 22 July 2013:

Dominic Needham, twelfth Marquis of Ranelagh, and his wife Laura, Lady Ranelagh, are delighted to announce the birth of their first child, a daughter, Mary.

Author's Note:

Those who read *A Hopeless Romantic*, to which this book is intended in part to be a sequel, might wonder at the timings of *Rules for Dating A Romantic Hero*. The first book was set in 2005, but to bring the story up to date for new readers (and to not leave Nick and Laura in limbo for such a long time) I have allowed four years to magically vanish. Author's prerogative!

I really hope you enjoyed this book.

Harriet xx

Books In The Series

Amy's Diary	Maureen Lee
Beyond the Bounty	Tony Parsons
Bloody Valentine	James Patterson
Blackout	Emily Barr
Chickenfeed	Minette Walters
Cleanskin	Val McDermid
The Cleverness of Ladies	Alexander McCall Smith
Clouded Vision	Linwood Barclay
A Cool Head	Ian Rankin
A Cruel Fate	Lindsey Davis
The Dare	John Boyne
Doctor Who: Code of the Krillitanes	Justin Richards
Doctor Who: Made of Steel	Terrance Dicks
Doctor Who: Magic of the Angels	Jacqueline Rayner
Doctor Who: Revenge of the Judoon	Terrance Dicks
Doctor Who: The Silurian Gift	Mike Tucker
Doctor Who: The Sontaran Games	Jacqueline Rayner
A Dreadful Murder	Minette Walters
A Dream Come True	Maureen Lee
The Escape	Lynda La Plante
Follow Me	Sheila O'Flanagan
Four Warned	Jeffrey Archer
Full House	Maeve Binchy
Get the Life You Really Want	James Caan
The Grey Man	Andy McNab
Hello Mum	Bernardine Evaristo
Hidden	Barbara Taylor Bradford

How to Change Your Life in 7 Steps	John Bird
Humble Pie	Gordon Ramsay
Jack and Jill	Lucy Cavendish
Kung Fu Trip	Benjamin Zephaniah
Last Night Another Soldier	Andy McNab
Life's New Hurdles	Colin Jackson
Life's Too Short	Val McDermid, Editor
Lily	Adèle Geras
The Little One	Lynda La Plante
Love is Blind	Kathy Lette
Men at Work	Mike Gayle
Money Magic	Alvin Hall
One Good Turn	Chris Ryan
The Perfect Holiday	Cathy Kelly
The Perfect Murder	Peter James
Quantum of Tweed: The Man with the Nissan Micra	Conn Iggulden
Raw Voices: True Stories of Hardship and Hope	Vanessa Feltz
Reading My Arse!	Ricky Tomlinson
Rules for Dating a Romantic Hero	Harriet Evans
A Sea Change	Veronica Henry
Star Sullivan	Maeve Binchy
Strangers on the 16:02	Priya Basil
Survive the Worst and Aim for the Best	Kerry Katona
The 10 Keys to Success	John Bird
Tackling Life	Charlie Oatway
Today Everything Changes	Andy McNab
Traitors of the Tower	Alison Weir
Trouble on the Heath	Terry Jones
Twenty Tales from the War Zone	John Simpson
We Won the Lottery	Danny Buckland
Wrong Time, Wrong Place	Simon Kernick

Lose yourself
in a good
book with **Galaxy**®

Curled up on the sofa,
Sunday morning in pyjamas,
just before bed,
in the bath or
on the way to work?

Wherever, whenever,
you can escape
with a good book!

So go on...
indulge yourself with
a good read and the
smooth taste of
Galaxy® chocolate.

Proudly supports **Quick Reads**

Quick Reads are brilliant short new books written by bestselling writers to help people discover the joys of reading for pleasure.

Find out more at **www.quickreads.org.uk**

 @Quick_Reads   Quick-Reads

We would like to thank all our funders:

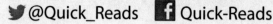
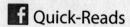

LOTTERY FUNDED

We would also like to thank all our partners in the Quick Reads project for their help and support: NIACE, unionlearn, National Book Tokens, The Reading Agency, National Literacy Trust, Welsh Books Council, The Big Plus Scotland, DELNI, NALA

At Quick Reads, World Book Day and World Book Night we want to encourage everyone in the UK and Ireland to read more and discover the joy of books.

World Book Day is on 6 March 2014
Find out more at **www.worldbookday.com**

World Book Night is on 23 April 2014
Find out more at **www.worldbooknight.org**

Start a new chapter

Hidden

Barbara Taylor Bradford

Drama, heartbreak and new beginnings.
This is a gripping story from a master storyteller.

On the surface, Claire Saunders has it all. She has a rewarding career in fashion and a talented concert pianist daughter. Her loving husband is one of the country's most trusted diplomats.

But every now and again, she has to plaster her face in heavy make-up and wears sunglasses. She thinks she's hidden her secret from her best friends, but they know her too well.

Can her friends get her out of harm's way and protect her from a man who is as ruthless as he is charming and powerful? And along the way, can Claire learn to stop protecting the wrong people?

Harper

Start a new chapter

Blackout

Emily Barr

You wake up in a strange room,
with no idea how you got there.

You are abroad, in a city you have never visited before.

You have no money, no passport, no phone.

And there is no sign of your baby.

What do you do?

Headline Review

Quick Reads

Start a new chapter

Rules for Dating a Romantic Hero

Harriet Evans

Do you believe in happy endings?

Laura Foster used to be a hopeless romantic. She was obsessed with meeting her own Prince Charming until she grew up and realised real life doesn't work like that.

Then she met Nick. A romantic hero straight from a fairytale, with a grand country estate and a family tree to match.

They've been together four years now and Laura can't imagine ever loving anyone the way she loves Nick.

Now, though, Nick is keeping secrets from Laura. She's starting to feel she might not be 'good enough' for his family.

Can an ordinary girl like Laura make it work with one of the most eligible men in the country?

Harper

Four Warned

Jeffrey Archer

These four short stories from a master storyteller
are packed full of twists and turns.

In Stuck on You, Jeremy steals the perfect ring for his fiancée.

Albert celebrates his 100th birthday, and is pleased
to be sent The Queen's Birthday Telegram.
Why hasn't his wife received hers?

In Russia, businessman Richard plots to murder his wife.
He thinks he's found the answer when his hotel
warns him: Don't Drink the Water.

Terrified for her life, Diana will do whatever it takes to stick to
the warning given to drivers: Never Stop on the Motorway …

Every reader will have their favourite story – some will make
you laugh, others will bring you to tears. And every
one of them will keep you spellbound.

Pan Books

Quick Reads

Start a new chapter

A Cruel Fate

Lindsey Davis

As long as war exists, this story will matter.

Martin Watts, a bookseller, is captured by the king's men.
Jane Afton's brother Nat is taken too. They both
suffer horrible treatment as prisoners-of-war.

In Oxford Castle jailer William Smith tortures, beats, starves
and deprives his helpless victims. Can Jane rescue her sick
brother before he dies of neglect? Will Martin dare to escape?

Based on real events in the English Civil War,
Lindsey Davis retells the grim tale of Captain Smith's
abuse of power in Oxford prison – where many
died in misery though a lucky few survived.

Hodder and Stoughton

Start a new chapter

The Escape

Lynda La Plante

Is a change of identity all it takes to leave prison?

Colin Burrows is desperate. Recently sent to prison
for burglary, he knows that his four-year sentence
means he will miss the birth of his first child.

Sharing a cell with Colin is Barry Marsden. Barry likes
prison life. He has come from a difficult family and been
in and out of foster homes all his life. In prison, he has three
meals a day and has discovered a talent for drawing.
He doesn't want to leave.

Sad to see his cellmate looking depressed, Barry hatches a plan
to get Colin out of jail for the birth. It's a plan so crazy
that it might just work.

**Bestselling author Lynda La Plante's exciting tale of one
man's escape from jail is based on a true story.**

Simon & Schuster

Why not start a reading group?

If you have enjoyed this book, why not share your next Quick Read with friends, colleagues, or neighbours.

A reading group is a great way to get the most out of a book and is easy to arrange. All you need is a group of people, a place to meet and a date and time that works for everyone.

Use the first meeting to decide which book to read first and how the group will operate. Conversation doesn't have to stick rigidly to the book. Here are some suggested themes for discussions:

- How important was the plot?

- What messages are in the book?

- Discuss the characters – were they believable and could you relate to them?

- How important was the setting to the story?

- Are the themes timeless?

- Personal reactions – what did you like or not like about the book?

There is a free toolkit with lots of ideas to help you run a Quick Reads reading group at **www.quickreads.org.uk**

Share your experiences of your group on Twitter @Quick_Reads

For more ideas, offers and groups to join visit Reading Groups for Everyone at **www.readingagency.org.uk/readinggroups**

Other resources

Enjoy this book?

Find out about all the others at **www.quickreads.org.uk**

For Quick Reads audio clips as well as videos
and ideas to help you enjoy reading visit the
BBC's Skillswise website **www.bbc.co.uk/quickreads**

Skillswise

Join the Reading Agency's Six Book Challenge at
www.readingagency.org.uk/sixbookchallenge

THE READING AGENCY

Find more books for new readers at
www.newisland.ie
www.barringtonstoke.co.uk

Free courses to develop your skills are available in your
local area. To find out more phone 0800 100 900.

For more information on developing your skills
in Scotland visit **www.thebigplus.com**

Want to read more? Join your local library. You can borrow
books for free and take part in inspiring reading activities.

Not without you, she said.
And I'd let her down . . .

Hollywood, 1961: when beautiful, much-loved movie star Eve Noel
vanishes at the height of her fame, no-one knows where, much less why.

Fifty years later, another young British actress, Sophie Leigh, lives in
Eve's house high in the Hollywood Hills. Eve Noel was her inspiration
and Sophie, disenchanted with her life in LA, finds herself increasingly
obsessed with the mystery of her idol's disappearance. And the more she
discovers, the more she realises Eve's life is linked with her own.

Sophie needs to unravel the truth to save them both –
but is she already too late? Becoming increasingly entangled in Eve's
world and as past and present start to collide, Sophie must decide
whose life she is really living . . .

'You'll race through the pages desperate to find out what happens'
Heat

'A multi-faceted tale of fading fame and shifting fortunes'
Grazia